DANGEROUS
AT HEART

Sandra Orchard

Annie's®
AnniesFiction.com

Books in the Sweet Intrigue series

Betrayal of Trust
Burning Danger
Christmas Peril
Dangerous at Heart
Web of Lies
Deceptive Truths
Fatal Waters

. . . and more to come!

Library of Congress-in-Publication Data
Dangerous at Heart / by Sandra Orchard
p. cm.
I. Title
             2020950290

AnniesFiction.com
(800) 282-6643
Annie's Sweet Intrigue™
Series Creator: Shari Lohner
Editors: Jane Haertel and Lorie Jones

10 11 12 13 14 | Printed in China | 9 8 7 6 5 4 3 2 1

The slow descent of Dr. Richard London's coffin into the earth roused more emotions than Laura Brennan could contain. Dabbing at her damp eyes, she edged away from the mourners. The doleful sound of a distant bagpipe brought a lump to her throat as painful memories clamored to be revisited. Everything in her longed to flee, but she managed to restrain her retreat to a sedate walk.

Instead of returning to her home as she longed to do, she ambled over the knoll toward the copse of aspens she knew too well. She'd been visiting her father's grave beneath the whispering boughs for more than fifteen years. And for the past few years, she'd managed not to think about the unknown carjacker who'd taken him from her. But witnessing Dr. London's fatal hit-and-run accident had resurrected the pain and her frustration that no one had ever been held accountable.

Laura rested her hand on the tombstone and dropped her head. Her dark hair fell over her face, the long curls concealing her tears from anyone who might happen by. A gentle breeze stirred the leaves overhead, carrying with it the last mournful note of the bagpiper's melody.

At the snap of a twig behind her, Laura immediately straightened and swiped the moisture from her cheeks.

Cold steel jabbed into her back, and a hand caught her by the shoulder. "Where is it?" demanded a gravelly male voice.

"I don't know what you're talking about." Her voice came out as scarcely more than a whisper. "You must have the wrong person."

"The file." His fingers dug into her shoulder, almost dropping her to her knees. "Don't play coy with me. You wouldn't be the first person I shot for not cooperating."

Her throat instantly dried. Why didn't he believe her?

"Ms. Brennan?" a much more pleasant male voice called from behind them.

Her assailant swung around, taking her with him.

Garrett Simons, Dr. London's nephew, whom she'd met in the receiving line at the visitation for his uncle, strode toward them. He appeared formidable in his army dress uniform.

Laura's assailant tightened his grip and hissed close to her ear, "I *will* find it." He shoved her toward Garrett and fled.

Garrett caught her by the arms. "Are you okay?"

"I am now," she said, straining to stop the wobble in her legs.

Garrett steadied her. "Wait here." He raced after her attacker, but the guy already had fifty yards on him.

An instant later, the assailant vaulted onto a motorcycle sitting curbside, revved it to life, and sped off.

Garrett headed back toward Laura, pulling his phone from his pocket and pressing the screen on the way. When he reached her side, he spoke into the phone. "Yes, an armed white male just attacked a woman at Rolling Meadows Cemetery and then left on a black motorcycle. First three characters of the license plate were 3S1." He paused, listening, then met Laura's gaze. "Do you know who your assailant was?"

"No idea," she answered. "He wanted a file he thought I had, but I didn't know what he was talking about. I think he must've mistaken me for someone else."

Garrett relayed her answer to the 911 dispatcher, then nodded and ended the call. "They're issuing a BOLO—be on the lookout—for the motorcycle, and they're sending an officer here to take your statement."

Wrapping her arms around her waist, Laura glanced around, suddenly feeling a little like a duck in a shooting gallery. And judging by the quickly dispersing crowd on the other side of the knoll, it would soon be an otherwise deserted gallery.

As if he'd sensed her thoughts, Garrett said, "You can sit in my car while we wait for the police."

At his kind offer, her heart slowed its rampaging gallop to a fast trot. She didn't know Garrett at all, but his presence was reassuring, and she was grateful she wouldn't have to wait alone.

He motioned toward a shiny black Subaru parked on the road that wound through the cemetery.

Laura allowed him to escort her down the slight incline toward the car. "I'm Laura Brennan, by the way." Her cheeks heated. "But I guess you already knew that, because you called out to me. I can't thank you enough."

"I'm glad I was here to help. I remember you from the visitation." Garrett cocked his head. "You're the owner of Dad's Diner, right?"

"Yes, that's me." She hadn't mentioned that fact to him last night. They hadn't spoken long since the entire town had turned out to extend condolences.

"My aunt spoke highly of you. She said you rushed to my uncle's aid after the hit-and-run accident."

Laura frowned. "I'm afraid there was little I could do. I'm so sorry for your loss."

Garrett nodded to acknowledge the sentiment he'd likely heard countless times over the past few days. "Doc was a good man. He was like a second father to me." His voice grew quiet. "We'd been making plans to share his practice when I left the army."

"Will you still move here?"

He sighed. "Yes, as soon as my discharge papers come through."

"I know it won't be the same without your uncle," she said. "But Hopeton is a beautiful place to live, and I'm sure it will comfort your aunt immensely to have you close by."

"I've had my fill of traveling the world. I'm looking forward to enjoying the quieter life of rural Pennsylvania." Garrett furrowed his brow. "Or at least, I thought it would be quieter."

"It usually is," she assured him, stifling a shudder at the thought of her assailant.

Six weeks later

Laura put on her straw hat and gardening gloves, then grabbed her bucket and tools from the shed and headed to the flower beds hugging the front of her brick bungalow. She paused in the driveway and lifted her face to the sunshine. With all the rain they'd been getting, she hadn't been able to enjoy nearly enough time in the garden this spring. And the recent break-in at the diner and subsequent repair work she'd had to oversee there hadn't helped.

She rolled her shoulders to shed the tension gripping them at the mere thought of the incident three weeks ago. Hopeton had never been a place where business owners had to worry about break-ins. Sure, the odd kid might filch a candy bar from the corner store, or the occasional tourist might slip out of the diner without paying after a visit to the restroom. But in all her thirty-two years, she couldn't remember a business being broken into at night. She shook her head and rolled her shoulders again. She'd come out here to de-stress, not brood all over again.

She glanced at Mrs. Forester's front flower bed next door. Only it wasn't Mrs. Forester's anymore. She'd moved out two weeks ago, and the new owner, Dr. Garrett Simons, hadn't yet moved in. Weeds now choked the beds Laura had kept in pristine order for all the open houses. She'd helped Mrs. Forester with her flower beds for years. This spring, after Mrs. Forester told her she'd be selling so she could move into an assisted living facility, Laura had planted a colorful assortment of annuals in the front bed to enhance the bungalow's curb appeal. It would be a shame for the new doctor to arrive and find them as shabby as the wood siding.

Laura wasn't sure the house would've been Garrett's first choice if Doc's death hadn't put such a severe dent in the time he'd had to search for a place. But with few houses in the area on the market and virtually no rentals available, his aunt had urged him to snatch it up while he could.

Laura's own front bed also needed attention, but she decided to spruce up her new neighbor's first. After Laura saw to the beds, maybe she'd mow both yards. Mrs. Forester must've canceled her contract with the company who'd been tending the lawn since her first ministroke two years ago because the grass was overgrown too. The cops had said kids looking for easy cash had likely been behind the diner break-in. A neglected lawn was like a banner proclaiming that no one was home.

The joke would be on the kids, since the place was empty. But the last thing Garrett needed to deal with was a broken window or a kicked-in door. Or worse, vandalism inside the house if the kids were frustrated that it was empty rather than full of valuables.

There she went again, thinking about the break-in. She dropped to her knees in front of the flower bed and yanked weeds, banishing thoughts of the burglary from her mind. Of course, that was easier said than done. The break-in had left her feeling vulnerable—again.

At least it had taken her mind off the assault at the cemetery. That had been totally unnerving. The cops hadn't been able to locate the motorcycle or its driver. The officer who took her report said there was no license plate in the state's database matching the numbers Garrett reported seeing. Since she wasn't hurt, the officer hadn't seemed inclined to question the owners with numbers close to it.

Laura would never forget the feeling of the gun that had been pressed into her ribs.

The cop, like her, had concluded the attack was a case of mistaken identity. And he had assured her the guy had realized his mistake and was likely long gone.

Still, it was comforting to know she'd soon have a former army officer living next door, even if his job had been doctoring, not soldiering. She visualized the man who had come to her rescue—sinewy arms, broad shoulders, and short dark hair with a few appealing gray strands at the temples. He was built like a soldier, and Laura was sure that any would-be intruder would think twice before putting the man's self-defense skills to the test.

The weeds removed, Laura fluffed the mulch, then traded her rake for her pruners and deadheaded the flowers. She wished she knew when Garrett was expected, because several of the blooms would last another day or so and then she'd have to be out here again.

She debated calling his aunt to ask, but she decided not to bother Jenny over such a trivial matter. The woman was preoccupied enough with dealing with her husband's estate and managing the medical clinic with the locum, the temporary doctor covering the practice until her nephew returned. Jenny had been so busy that she'd stopped by the diner only once in the six weeks since her husband's funeral.

Or maybe it wasn't busyness that kept her away. It had to be hard to return to places she'd once enjoyed with her spouse. It had been that way when Laura lost her dad. Her parents had run the diner before he'd been killed. Even now, she almost expected him to step out from behind the grill to greet her when she went to work.

She shook the memory from her mind and refocused on the flower bed in front of her. Perhaps she'd clip the fullest blooms and arrange them in a vase. That way, if her new neighbor arrived in the next day or two, she could present him with the flowers to spruce up his kitchen table. If he didn't, then at least she wouldn't have to worry about deadheading again until Monday.

Laura snipped a few daisies, several yellow pansies, and a couple of orange gerberas, then assessed the size of the bundle of stems. Deciding she could fit a few more into the vase she planned to use, she scanned the bed for candidates.

A police cruiser pulled into her driveway.

Her breath quickened. *Maybe there's been a development in the burglary investigation.* Recognizing Lieutenant Elliott Reynolds as he exited his car, she called out, "I'm over here. On my way." She leaned down and tossed her tools on top of her weed bucket to carry it back to her house.

Not bothering to wait for her to come to him, the six-foot-three lieutenant traipsed across the lawn and shoved a copy of a driver's license photo at her. "This is the man you saw run down Dr. London."

"What?" Was he asking her or telling her? Laura released her hold on the bucket and clutched the bouquet of flowers she'd cut. "You're not here about the burglary at the diner?" Okay, stupid question. He wouldn't be asking about Dr. London's hit-and-run driver if he was. She studied the photo. "No, I don't think this is the man I saw."

"Look again." Reynolds held it closer to her as if that would make a difference. "We found the vehicle that ran London down. This is the man who was extricated from the wreck."

Laura shook her head. She could clearly picture the face of the young man behind the wheel of the street-racing pickup. The guy in the photo wasn't him.

"You're mistaken," he insisted, his voice akin to a snarling dog.

"No, I remember him clearly."

The officer snorted, his features growing steelier by the second. "You'd only have seen him for a second or two, and that was close to seven weeks ago." He waved the photo at her. "*This* is the guy who was driving the pickup."

Laura recoiled at the animosity radiating from him as he attempted to "refresh" her memory.

"He fits the description you gave us, as does the truck we recovered. And preliminary forensics confirm the man has been dead for six to seven weeks."

Laura wavered. Could she be wrong? Driver's license photos weren't always a great likeness of people. She squinted again at the image. But she couldn't convince herself to say yes, not when her gut told her the man in the picture wasn't Doc's killer.

Of course, the lieutenant wanted him to be the guy, because then there'd be no need for a trial. Case closed.

But detectives had bungled the investigation into her own father's murder, and she wasn't about to let them cut corners on this one. Not if it meant Doc's killer could still be out there somewhere.

Lieutenant Reynolds clasped her arm. "The last thing the grieving family needs is the press churning up more speculation because our eyewitness's memory is foggy."

Laura tried to tug back her arm, but she couldn't break his grasp. "My memory is *not* foggy. I know what I saw."

"Now you listen to me." His grip tightened, and his voice dropped to a sinister pitch. "Don't you dare speak to anyone about this investigation."

Garrett Simons couldn't believe it. The young woman who was stealing his flowers was the same woman who'd witnessed his uncle's accident. And once again some goon was bothering her—except this goon was a police officer.

Garrett slammed his car door. "Hey, what's going on here?"

The officer released his hold on Laura's arm. He said something to her, then turned on his heel and stalked to his car.

Laura gaped at the officer as he peeled away with a screech of tires, her gaze as wild as the long curls that had escaped her ponytail.

Garrett reached her side. "Are you okay?"

Her smile sent a shot of warmth straight through him. "Rescuing me from bullies is becoming a habit of yours. Thank you."

To his surprise, she sounded unfazed by the encounter. He searched her face for evidence to the contrary, resisting the urge to thumb away the adorable dirt smudge on the tip of her nose. "I take it he wasn't citing you for pilfering pansies?" He gestured toward the bouquet in her hands.

Laura scrutinized the flowers, and a lovely shade of pink colored her high cheekbones. "No." She held the flowers out to him. "I picked them for you. I was weeding and deadheading the bed, and I wasn't sure when you were—" She abruptly stopped talking, as if she'd sensed she was babbling.

As Garrett accepted the flowers, his fingers grazed her wrist, and he couldn't help but notice she was trembling. So the cop *had* unnerved her. Garrett surveyed the bucket full of weeds and dead flower heads. "You did all that for me?" To think moments ago, he'd been doubting the friendly small-town vibe his real estate agent had boasted about the place.

"Of course. I wanted the gardens to be in good shape when you arrived. I used to help Mrs. Forester with them. I love gardening."

Mesmerized by the passion in her voice, he studied her in a new light. "But you run a diner." Before she could respond, he shook his head. "First things first. What did that officer want? Why was he threatening you?"

Laura was clearly taken aback by his perception of their exchange. "He didn't threaten me."

"It sure looked like it from where I stood. Was he here about the guy who assaulted you at the cemetery?" A chill sliced through him at the reminder. Laura Brennan had invaded his thoughts frequently since that day, and he'd wondered if she'd had any more trouble.

She winced but didn't reply.

Garrett touched her arm. "Did they find the guy?"

"No, that's not why the lieutenant came. I'm not supposed to talk about it."

"Why not?"

"He warned me not to, because he didn't want the press speculating and distressing Dr. London's family."

"I *am* Dr. London's family. If this concerns my uncle's death, I want to know about it." He realized he'd raised his voice and made a point of gentling it before adding, "I'm not the press."

Laura nodded. "I'm sure they've told your aunt already anyway."

"Told her what?"

"They think they've located the pickup that hit your uncle. The driver was still behind the wheel. Dead. For six or seven weeks, they figure. I guess they assume he crashed the truck sometime after hitting your uncle. I'm not sure. I didn't get a chance to ask."

"Do they want you to go in and ID the driver?" Garrett cringed at the thought. He'd been around enough dead bodies to know how gut-wrenching it could be. And a seven-week-old corpse would be badly decayed.

"No." A note of surprise tinged her response, as if she'd only now realized that would've been the logical request. "The officer didn't say anything like that. He showed me the guy's driver's license photo." She pressed her lips together and went silent.

"What's wrong?"

Laura grimaced, clearly reluctant to voice what was bothering her. After a long exhalation, she finally said, "The guy in the photo wasn't the driver I saw."

He raised his eyebrows. "You're sure?"

She shrugged. "Not completely. Lieutenant Reynolds clearly wants to close the case with a tidy bow and be done with it, but I'm not convinced they've got your uncle's killer."

Garrett started to understand where the officer's anger might have come from. Not that that excused it. The man had a duty to follow the evidence and keep an open mind when the evidence—including eyewitnesses' identifications—didn't fit into the neat little box he thought he'd found. Now the officer had more work to do. "I appreciate your fortitude in standing by your convictions, given the pressure he was exerting on you to agree."

Garrett wasn't sure which disturbed him more—the fact that Laura didn't think the man found inside the recovered pickup was the driver she'd seen or that the cop had told her not to tell anyone.

"I want to see justice served," she said.

Garrett nodded. "Me too."

Laura attempted to close her conversation with Garrett and edge toward her yard at the sight of Beth Wise jogging up the street. The town librarian had been Laura's best friend for as long as she could remember, but now that Beth was engaged, Beth's matchmaking radar always shifted into high alert the instant she spotted Laura even looking at a man. And when said man was holding a bouquet of flowers, who could say where her thoughts would spiral?

Beth veered off the sidewalk and jogged across his yard toward them. She tugged the earbuds from her ears and beamed at Laura.

Laura glared at her friend and mouthed, "Don't embarrass me."

"Welcome to Hopeton, Doc," Beth said.

"Beth, isn't it?" Garrett asked.

Laura was impressed he'd remembered her too, given how many new people he'd met at his uncle's funeral. Then again, her friend's bubbly personality and gorgeous long blonde hair were pretty memorable.

"That's right. Beth Wise, soon to become Beth Wright." She grinned, never able to resist an opportunity to enjoy the fun play on words of her and her fiancé's surnames. "I came to find out if Laura heard they found the truck that ran down your uncle, but I guess the cop I saw driving away filled you both in."

"How did *you* hear about it?" Garrett asked.

Beth swept aside her hand as if to assure him the whole town wasn't already gossiping about it. "Ryan, my fiancé, is a volunteer firefighter. He helped with the truck's extrication. It was partially sunk in a marshy area on Exeter Road outside of town. A couple of hikers happened upon it and reported it."

"I wonder why the officer didn't tell us that," Garrett mused. He returned his attention to Laura. "Thank you for freshening up my flower beds." He raised the bouquet she'd given him. "And for these. I'll see you again soon."

"Anytime you need a hand with your plants," Laura said, "don't hesitate to give me a shout."

"Gardening is kind of her thing," Beth explained.

"So I gathered." He smiled. "Here I thought it would be cooking."

Laura blinked. "I like cooking too."

"She inherited the diner—"

Laura tugged Beth's arm before she could launch into a lengthy explanation of how Laura had wound up running a diner. "It's not important. Let's go so the man can settle in."

"Would you like a hand carrying boxes in from your truck?" Beth volunteered.

Amusement danced in Garrett's exquisite blue eyes. "No thanks. I don't have much with me today. Most of my belongings are still in storage."

Laura steered Beth toward her house before her friend could come up with another reason to stall their departure.

This time Beth acquiesced with a wave for Garrett and said, "Nice meeting you again."

"You've got to stop doing this to me," Laura hissed as they crossed her driveway.

"Doing what?" Beth asked, her tone a little too innocent.

"Keep trying to set me up. Don't think I didn't notice." It wasn't as if she didn't see the appeal. Garrett was clearly handsome and very nice, not to mention gallant.

Beth laughed. "Was it that obvious?"

"Oh yeah. Come on. I'll get you a glass of lemonade."

The roar of a passing motorcycle yanked Laura's attention to the street. Her heart stuttered at the sight of a man in a dark sedan parked two houses down. He was watching them. She'd noticed the sedan pull up soon after the cop arrived. She'd assumed it was someone visiting her neighbor, not someone spying on her. Why would anyone want to spy on her?

Her thoughts turned to the attack in the cemetery and the break-in at her diner. She shifted her focus to the license plate, but the man raced off before she could read it, as if he sensed her purpose.

Laura pushed her friend up the porch steps toward the front door. "Get inside."

"What's wrong?" Beth asked.

"I'm not sure. Did you notice the dark sedan on the other side of the street when you got here?"

Beth glanced over her shoulder. "No. Why?"

"I think he was watching us. Or the house."

"Seriously?" Beth spun around.

"He's gone now." Laura set her bucket of tools and clippings on the porch and nudged Beth inside.

"I don't like it," Beth said. "First the assault at the cemetery, then the break-in at your diner. Now someone's watching you?"

"The police didn't think the assault and break-in were connected." Laura should trust the police on this, right? She opened the fridge and stared at the contents, straining for a moment to remember why she'd opened it.

"You were getting us lemonade," Beth prompted. "I think it's a mistake for the police to dismiss the possibility that the two incidents are connected. After all, you said the guy at the cemetery asked you where something was. Maybe he broke into the diner to find it."

Laura handed Beth a tall glass. "A month later?"

Beth followed Laura to the sunny front room and sat in the armchair by the one window that offered a view of Garrett's driveway. "Maybe the guy was waiting for you to let down your guard."

"Are you trying to cheer me up?" Laura's voice oozed exasperation. "Because you're doing a horrible job."

"Sorry. But you've got to admit it's freaky."

"You don't have to remind me. I'm the one living it." Laura sat in the chair facing Beth's and debated whether to defy the cop's warning a second time.

Beth, who was abnormally interested in the window, said, "I think you made a great first impression on your hunky new neighbor. Tending to his flowers when he was due to arrive was a stroke of genius."

"More like dumb luck."

Beth flashed Laura a victorious grin. "So, you admit you like him?"

"He seems like a good guy. But the last thing I want you to do is push us together. I don't want to move."

Beth drew back, her forehead creasing. "Why would you have to move?"

"To avoid uncomfortable meetings when the relationship doesn't work out."

Beth shook her head. "You're such a pessimist."

"No, I'm a realist. And I'm happy with my life the way it is."

"If you say so." Beth shot one last look out the window, then curled her feet under her legs in her chair, as if snuggling up in preparation for a good story. "So, do you have to go to the morgue to ID the driver they pulled out of the pickup?"

"Not that I was told, no."

"What did they do? Bring you a picture of him?"

"Hmmm." Laura sipped her lemonade.

"That's all I get?"

"The cop told me I wasn't supposed to talk about the case."

"Why?"

"He didn't want the press to warp the story and upset Dr. London's family further."

"What's to warp?" Beth's eyes suddenly widened. She set her glass down and leaned toward Laura, planting her feet on the floor. "You don't think the dead guy is the hit-and-run driver, do you?"

Laura abruptly drew back. "What makes you say that?"

Beth smirked. "Your reaction for one. Also, Ryan overheard one of the state troopers say the truck was reported stolen the same day as Dr. London's accident."

"Really?" Now why had the investigator neglected to mention that fact to Laura?

"Didn't the cop tell you the body they pulled from the wreckage wasn't the truck's owner?"

Laura shook her head. What else were the police withholding?

Beth rubbed her hands together, clearly beginning to imagine theories, as if this were a case in one of her favorite detective novels instead of Laura's life. "After the accident, maybe the real owner, petrified of being found out, abandoned his truck and reported it stolen, hoping the police would assume that the thief barreled through town, taking out Dr. London in his rush to escape."

Laura shuddered. The theory made sense. Were the police simply too eager to close the case to consider it?

"Then again," Beth mused, "what are the chances the thief would fit your description of the driver?"

"Dumb luck?" Laura proposed.

"Maybe. Or maybe the real perp staged the accident on Exeter Road as some kind of elaborate cover-up."

Laura frowned. "Where would he have gotten the dead body for the driver's seat?"

"Some homeless guy?"

"A homeless guy with a current driver's license in his wallet? I think you've been reading too many novels." Laura sighed. She was starting to see why the investigator didn't want her talking about her certainty that the driver wasn't their man.

But her gut still said he wasn't. So maybe Beth's crazy theories weren't all that far from the truth.

The next morning Garrett drove to Dad's Diner to meet Aunt Jenny for breakfast to discuss his pending takeover of his uncle's medical practice. From their conversations on the phone since the funeral, Garrett had the impression she was coping with the loss of her husband by throwing all her energy into overseeing a smooth transition for his patients. Garrett hoped his aunt wouldn't feel so adrift once she handed over the clinic's helm.

He nabbed a parking spot in front of the diner as a patron pulled out, and he couldn't help but notice the long window box overflowing with a cheerful array of orange and yellow flowers—Laura's handiwork, no doubt. He opened the diner's door and was greeted by the jingle of an overhead bell.

"Let me clear this—" Laura glanced up from the table she'd started wiping. Aside from lip gloss, she wore no makeup, not that she needed any. "Oh, Garrett, it's you." She picked up the coffeepot she'd set down and backstepped to the booth she'd been serving. "Your aunt's right here. Coffee?"

"Yes, thank you." He slid into the seat across from Jenny.

Laura flipped his cup upright in its saucer and poured him some coffee. "How are you this morning? Have you settled into your new place okay?"

"Yes, and your flowers made a cheery addition to my kitchen," Garrett said.

"I'm glad to hear it." Laura smiled, then motioned to the dispenser on the table. "The menus are there. Let me know when you're ready to order."

"Will do. Thanks." He returned his attention to his aunt, who was smiling at him with a peculiar glint in her gaze. "What?"

Jenny shook her head. "Just happy to see you."

He leaned over and gave her a peck on the cheek. "I'm happy to see you too. How are *you* doing?"

She shrugged and sipped her coffee. "As well as can be expected."

He nodded solemnly.

"I already know what I'm ordering." Jenny pulled a menu out of the dispenser and passed it to him. "Laura says you're a quiet neighbor."

"As is she. I was a little taken aback when I arrived to find her making off with a bouquet from my front garden," he said wryly.

His aunt chuckled. "She mentioned that. She does love her flowers." She motioned to the pint-size arrangements of fresh blooms on each table around the diner—far cheerier than the typical plastic fare of the truck stops he'd hit on his drive across the country.

"I'm surprised she works in a diner," Garrett remarked. "From what I saw of the gardens at her house, she clearly has a green thumb and an eye for design."

"She inherited this restaurant from her parents. I suspect the notion of letting it go is hard to contemplate."

Understanding his new neighbor a little better, Garrett studied the menu. Jenny seemed to know Laura as more than a passing acquaintance—or maybe that was simply the reality of small-town living. He debated how to learn even more without raising his aunt's curiosity. He wasn't sure himself why he was interested. His new house needed umpteen updates, and he was taking over his uncle's busy medical practice. It wasn't as if Garrett had time to date anyone. He closed the menu.

"What are you ordering?" Jenny asked.

Realizing he hadn't actually looked at the options, he reopened the menu. "Number one sounds good."

A quirky smile flashed across his aunt's lips as she flagged down Laura. "Two number ones, please."

"You got it," Laura called, bustling toward the kitchen with a tray of dirty dishes.

Jenny pressed her hands to the table. "Okay, now down to business. I've contracted with the temporary doctor, who's been seeing your uncle's patients, for another two weeks to give you time to settle into your house and acquaint yourself with the office."

"Sounds good. How are patients responding to the transition?"

"To be honest, I think a lot of them have been putting off their regular visits, perhaps waiting for you or for the dust to settle. Or they're uncomfortable with the fact that Dr. Henri"—she pronounced the name *On-ree*—"is a woman."

"Men need to get over that," he said decisively. "I would've thought a lot of Uncle Richard's female patients might prefer a woman."

"Except Isabelle is a tall, dark-haired beauty with a gorgeous French accent. She doesn't quite fit most people's image of a local doc."

Garrett excused himself to visit the restroom. By the time he returned, Laura was at their table with their breakfasts. She turned to leave, her expression as haunted as when she'd recounted what she'd witnessed the day of his uncle's accident. He knew the visage too well, often catching it staring back at him from the mirror.

Laura hurried past him without making eye contact.

Oddly disappointed, Garrett slid into his seat.

His aunt pushed aside a newly arrived newspaper, her hand trembling.

"What's wrong?" he asked.

Jenny worked her jaw, appearing to struggle to contain her emotions.

What could Laura have said that had left his aunt so distressed?

Jenny flipped the newspaper over and pointed to the headline: *Justice for Dr. London.*

"Is this the first you've heard?" Garrett reached across the table and squeezed her hand. It was cold, too cold. "The police never told you yesterday?" What was wrong with them, letting a victim's widow hear about such a big break in the case this way? He could kick himself for not calling her yesterday after she'd texted him the time of their breakfast meeting.

Jenny slipped her hand from his and dabbed at her eyes with a napkin. "They did, but they never told me the truck was stolen. There's no mention of it in the article. But Laura told me that Beth's fiancé said the driver wasn't the truck's owner. Laura said she called the police to attempt to confirm if the rumor is true, but they aren't returning her calls."

Garrett gritted his teeth, annoyed with Laura for burdening his aunt with this hearsay. Never mind how much he'd admired her fortitude in not simply complying with the officer's expectation that she'd ID the driver so he could close the case.

"I'm sure the police are doing everything in their power to ensure they have the right man," Garrett said. "The reporter must've chosen not to give credence to the unsubstantiated rumor for a reason, don't you think?" He recalled the officer's edict to Laura—one he'd perhaps given the reporter too.

Jenny took several deep breaths. "You're right. Of course." She piled eggs and bacon onto her toast, then sliced off a bite. But before she could bring it to her mouth, her cell phone rang. She checked the screen. "It's the office. I should take it."

Garrett took the opportunity to catch Laura at a nearby table she was clearing. "Listen, I know the cop who came to see you yesterday really bothered you, but I'd appreciate it in the future if you'd come to me with any concerns or new information about the investigation instead of my aunt."

Laura bristled.

Okay, that had come out a lot harsher than he'd meant it to. "It's just that your revelation distressed her, and I want to protect her from that as much as I can."

Laura nodded. "I understand. I thought the police would have told her, even if they didn't tell me. I'm sorry I upset her."

"So, next time you'll come to me before going to my aunt?" he pressed.

"I can do that."

"Thanks," Garrett said.

His aunt suddenly bolted from her seat and gathered her things.

Garrett reached the table as she tossed a twenty on it. "What's going on?"

"I've got to go. There's been a break-in at the office."

"I'll drive you." He mentally calculated the bill for their meals, then reached into his pocket and added a few dollars to the table to bolster the tip. "Sorry, but we've got to go," Garrett said by way of explanation as Laura hurried toward them.

"If you can wait a second, I'll box your food."

"No, you've already done enough."

Laura stared after Garrett as he accompanied his aunt outside. He had a lot of nerve talking to her like that. She'd thought he was so nice. But she should've known better from the way he'd demanded she run any notion she had concerning the investigation by him before going to his aunt, whom she'd known since she was in knee socks.

"Two number twos are up," Tom Nelson called from the kitchen's service window.

Laura shook thoughts of Garrett from her head. She thanked the cook, picked up the meals, and carried them to table seven. But table seven already had their plates. She glanced around until she found a table with two meal-less customers. "Two number twos?" she asked as pleasantly as she could.

"That's us, dear." White-haired Mrs. MacKenzie fluttered open her paper napkin and placed it across her lap. "Don't forget Herbert's prune juice."

Her husband grimaced. He clearly hated the stuff, but he always dutifully drank it whenever his wife remembered to order it for him.

When Laura returned with Herbert's juice, Mrs. MacKenzie said, "Isn't it sad how trouble upon trouble is befalling poor Doc London's wife? First the doc's death and now the burglary."

Laura's pulse quickened. "What burglary?"

"At the clinic," Mrs. MacKenzie replied. "I overheard Jenny tell her nephew about it right before they dashed out of here."

Laura wondered if that was why Garrett had been so abrupt with her. She knew all too well how unsettling the personal violation of the crime felt. Maybe he hadn't meant his parting comment the way it had sounded.

There she went again, making excuses for yet another control freak. Being upset was one thing. Taking it out on her was him being a jerk.

"I hope her nephew is as good a doctor as Doc London," Herbert chimed in. "This woman they got filling in for him is useless."

"Herbert!" Mrs. MacKenzie scolded.

"It's true. When I started getting one weird symptom after another, the doc worked hard to figure out what was causing them. This woman says it's all in my head and prescribes an ineffective pill."

A middle-aged woman sitting at the table across the aisle from him said, "You too? My daughter's friend came down with an unusual rash and a few other odd symptoms, and Dr. Henri told her mother the girl was depressed and needed medication."

"Same with me," Herbert echoed.

"Which is ridiculous," Mrs. MacKenzie interjected. "I've been married to the man for sixty years, and I've never seen him depressed a day in my life."

Herbert chugged his juice and chuckled. "Except for the twenty seconds a day it takes me to down her infernal prune juice. Otherwise, the only reason I'd feel depressed is because no one can give me an explanation that makes sense for my sudden health issues."

"You *are* eighty-five," his wife reminded him.

"My dad lived to be ninety-five without so much as an earache."

Laura refilled Herbert's coffee cup. "Garrett—Dr. Simons—seems as if he'll be a conscientious doctor."

"I hope you're right," Herbert said, then dug into the bacon and eggs Laura suspected he'd been eating for all of his eighty-plus years, even during the decades when experts were against the meal due to its high cholesterol levels.

Thankfully most of Hopeton's townsfolk paid no heed to the latest diet fads that would banish eggs from their menu one year and pancakes and French toast the next. But Laura always had a selection of fresh fruit and creamy oatmeal on hand in case she had a health-conscious customer.

After the morning rush subsided, Laura cleared and cleaned the tables for the impending influx of lunch customers.

Beth poked her head through the door. "Have time for a coffee break with me?"

"Sounds like a perfect idea." Laura poured them each a mug and heaved an exhausted sigh as she joined her friend at the table.

"Sounds like you had a rough morning."

Laura shrugged.

"So, I guess your new neighbor didn't visit the diner today." Beth leaned back in her chair and rested her feet on the one next to it, grinning.

"I wish he hadn't."

"What?" Beth's feet thudded to the floor as she jerked upright. "What happened?"

"He was a jerk." Laura told Beth about how annoyed he'd gotten with her about upsetting his aunt and how he'd topped that off with his refusal of her offer to box their order to go, claiming she'd already done enough.

"Are you sure you didn't take it the wrong way?" Beth asked. "Ever since you gave Mel an ultimatum, you've tended to see a controlling nature in every guy you've dated."

Laura sipped her coffee. She really didn't want to discuss her former boyfriend with Beth right now. In fact, she didn't even want to think about Mel Tanner.

"When people are stressed, they can be domineering in an attempt to get their emotions under control. I've seen it with Ryan when he's had a grueling fire to manage."

"I'm sure he doesn't take it out on you."

"You know what I think?" Beth asked.

Laura waited, knowing Beth would tell her whether Laura wanted to hear it or not.

"I think for his comment to get you this annoyed, you must already like him a little bit, or you'd shake it off like you do those truckers who ask you on a date every time they traipse through town."

"No, he's my neighbor. I wanted him to be likable. There's a difference."

"I'm sure when he has time to reflect on his reaction, he'll feel like a worm for the way he spoke to you. In the meantime, you need to take the high road. Let him see how wrong he was."

Laura savored another sip of her coffee. "You could be right."

Tom cleared his throat, then spoke up from the kitchen's pass-through window. "I'm making myself a grilled cheese sandwich. You want one?" The cook was a little rough around the edges. His shaved head and tattooed arms didn't help the image any, but deep down, he was a marshmallow.

Beth glanced at her watch. "I can't. I've got to get back to work." She squeezed Laura's shoulder. "Think about what I said."

"I will." Laura collected the coffee mugs and turned to Tom. "I'd love a grilled cheese, please. While you're at it, could you make a couple of turkey club sandwiches?"

Tom nodded.

"I want to take a nice brunch over to Jenny and her nephew, since they didn't get a chance to eat their breakfasts," Laura explained. She pulled the strawberry pie from the display case and transferred two slices to a to-go box.

Twenty minutes later, Laura parked in the medical clinic's lot, checked her hair in the visor mirror, then carried in the brunch boxes Tom had helped her prepare. *Take the high road.*

A *Closed* sign hung on the door.

Laura knocked anyway. When no one answered, she tested the knob. It wasn't locked, so she pushed it open. "Hello? It's Laura." She stepped inside. The reception area was a disaster. Desk drawers lay on the floor, contents strewn everywhere. Wires dangled from the desk where a computer used to sit.

Jenny bustled in from a back room.

"They stole your computer?" Laura was aghast at the mess.

"We had one in each of the exam rooms," Jenny said. "They took them all."

"They?"

"They, he, whoever it was." Jenny shrugged. "The police don't have a clue. They lifted a few fingerprints from the desk drawers, but they didn't seem hopeful they'd help. They said they never got any prints that couldn't be accounted for from your burglary. Is that true?"

Laura's pulse quickened. "Do they think this is the work of the same person?"

"I imagine." Jenny eyed the to-go boxes. "You brought us food? You're a dear. My stomach has been grumbling all morning."

Laura handed her one of the boxes. "It's the least I could do. On the house."

"Garrett," Jenny called toward the exam rooms, "Laura brought us sustenance."

Laura stiffened and pasted a smile on her face.

Garrett arrived, looking disheveled. His gaze met hers, then skittered away. "This is really nice of you." He smiled sheepishly.

Humph. Laura handed him the box. "I don't like to see anyone go hungry," she said sweetly.

"Okay, okay. I was a jerk earlier."

His aunt stifled a snort.

Laura remained silent. Who was she to argue with a doctor's diagnosis?

"I'm sorry," Garrett said.

The high road isn't so bad. Laura let him dangle a moment before nodding. "Apology accepted." She scanned the room once more. "Did the police say anything to you about this possibly being the work of the same person who burglarized the diner?"

"They mentioned that burglary," Garrett said. "I'm sorry you had to go through that."

Jenny's phone rang. She excused herself and went in the direction of the kitchenette.

Garrett motioned toward Doc's old office at the end of a short hallway. "Do you have a sec?"

"Sure." Laura followed him into the room and sat down on the chair he cleared for her.

"Did my aunt tell you all the office computers were stolen?"

"Yes. My thief made a similar mess of my office, but he only took our petty cash. He left the computer behind. Of course, it's old. A thief probably couldn't pay someone to take it off his hands."

Garrett sat behind his uncle's desk—now his desk. "Computers can easily be replaced. Our bigger concern is the patient records they contained."

"Surely you have backups."

Garrett raked his fingers through his hair. "The backup drive was stolen too. We're concerned what the thief might do with the information."

"Hopefully he was just after the computers." Laura winced at the magnitude of the missing information—extremely private information. "Did you have any kind of cloud-based backups?"

A woman, presumably the locum, walked past the door.

Garrett rose and closed it. "Apparently the automatic backup protocol has been corrupted for some time and none of the staff noticed."

"Not good."

"Tell me about it." He lowered his voice. "Our one saving grace is that my aunt did a manual backup of the entire database onto a jump drive she gave me six weeks ago so I could acquaint myself with the practice's patients."

"That's great. So you simply have to rebuild the patients' records from the past six weeks."

"I'd rather no one else knows about it yet."

Laura cocked her head, surprised that he'd shared the information with her.

"I didn't even tell the cops," he went on, "because I got to thinking about the guy who grabbed you at the cemetery."

Her breath caught in her throat. "Why?" She wiped her suddenly clammy hands on her pants.

"He wanted something from you, remember?"

Too well. Laura straightened, feeling the jab of the gun in her back once more.

"Then your diner was ransacked and now my uncle's clinic."

"You think the burglar is still searching for whatever he thought I had?"

Garrett nodded. "Since you were the first person on the scene after the hit-and-run accident, I'm guessing whatever this guy is trying to find had to do with my uncle. Did Doc give you anything before he died?"

"No. He was barely conscious by the time I got to him."

"Did he say anything about a file or another item someone would want?"

Laura mentally revisited Doc's last tragic moments. "No. I told him an ambulance was on its way and that he'd be okay. He said, 'You have to stop—' Then he struggled to breathe. I assumed he wanted me to stop his bleeding, so I applied pressure to the wound and urged him to stay quiet and save his strength." She swiped a tear from her cheek. "He said a few other garbled things. Nothing about a file."

"Can you recall his exact words?" Garrett pressed.

"He said something like 'the drums.' He wasn't making any sense."

"You're sure he said 'drums'?"

Laura shrugged. "That's what it sounded like. The paramedics arrived, and he said, 'You have to make them stop.' I thought his head must be pounding in pain. It broke my heart to see him so confused."

Garrett sighed, clearly disturbed by her account as well.

Laura glanced at the clock behind his desk. "I need to go. The lunch crowd will be arriving soon."

Garrett pushed to his feet. "Thank you again for lunch. I owe you one."

"That's okay. That's what neighbors do."

Garrett turned the door handle. Before opening the door, he said in a hushed voice, "Keep our conversation between us for now."

Responding to his tone of authority, she saluted. "Understood."

He grinned at her.

As Laura walked through the reception area, Jenny stopped her to introduce Dr. Henri. The woman reminded her of a movie star and seemed almost as aloof as Laura imagined a famous actress would be.

Then again, the woman's gaze tracked Garrett's retreat to his office before returning to Laura, so perhaps she had a secret crush on the new doctor and saw Laura as competition.

Oh brother, now I'm starting to sound like Beth.

Nevertheless, Laura could see why the townsfolk were having a difficult time warming to the interim doctor. Laura extended her hand. "Nice to meet you. I'm the owner of Dad's Diner. Stop by sometime for coffee and a muffin on the house."

"That's a kind offer. Thank you." The woman's smile transformed her aloof persona into something much more personable, making Laura glad she'd extended the invitation.

Laura felt a little sorry for Dr. Henri. The woman was probably shy rather than standoffish, but because of the vibe she gave off, she likely hadn't made many friends since moving to town.

Back at the diner, the lunch rush was busier than usual, and the next couple of hours passed in a blur.

After the last customer exited, Laura didn't even wait until she'd finished clearing tables before pouring herself a decaf coffee and sitting down.

Tom poured himself one and joined her. "Still not sleeping?"

She'd confided in him a couple of days ago that she'd had trouble sleeping since the break-in. Well, if she were completely honest with herself, since the attack at the cemetery. "The bags under my eyes getting that bad?"

"No. I guess this latest burglary has you nervous again?"

"Something like that. The lieutenant didn't return my call when I was out, did he?"

"Nope. What is it you're after him about?"

Laura hesitated. The cop had warned her not to share her doubts about the driver with anyone. But between Beth guessing correctly and Laura not being able to stop herself from asking Jenny if the cops had said anything to her about the dead driver, Laura wasn't exactly toeing the line in that regard. She blew out a long breath, then shared her reservations about the dead driver not being the person who'd struck Doc.

Tom whistled. "Let's hope you're wrong."

"Why?"

"Because someone who'd resort to supplying a corpse to cover up his crime might not stop there if he hears the cops' star witness isn't playing ball."

Once Laura had finished mopping the diner floor for the day, she used the phone behind the counter to dial the lieutenant's number. If he wasn't going to call her back, she'd annoy him with messages until he changed his mind. After Beth had left the night before, Laura had managed to convince herself the corpse was merely the victim of his own car-stealing stupidity, but fat chance she'd be able to get Tom's scenario out of her head.

"This is Lieutenant Reynolds. How may I help you?"

"You answered." Laura reiterated the earlier messages she'd left.

"Yes, we've confirmed that the truck was the vehicle that struck Dr. London. I can assure you that the driver you saw that day was the man we recovered, not the truck's owner. They look nothing alike."

"Since I'm the eyewitness, why don't you let me be the judge of that?"

"Because the owner is a 256-pound bald guy."

She deflated at that news. "You've seen him."

"Yes, and our thief has a record for drug possession and driving under the influence," Reynolds said. "Chances are he was doing just that at the time the accident happened—both accidents. Trust me, the case is closed. We couldn't have asked for better justice for Dr. London."

Laura tightened her grip on the phone's receiver. She wished she could believe that. She really did. But the dead guy wasn't the driver she'd seen. Straining to keep her tone sounding pleasantly curious, she said, "May I ask the name of the truck's owner?"

"Sorry, but that information is privileged. Have a good day."
The lieutenant disconnected before she could say anything more.

She repeated the conversation to Tom.

The cook shook his head. "The guy sounds like a jerk. I'm sorry I opened my big mouth and got you all upset for nothing."

"Didn't you hear me? It doesn't matter that the truck's owner couldn't have been who I saw. Maybe he's trying to protect someone else, his son or brother who borrowed the truck or something. All I know is the guy who ran down Doc wasn't the guy they recovered from the pickup."

Tom pulled his grease-smeared apron over his head and wadded it into a ball. "You *think*."

The terrible image flashed through her mind. She could still picture the driver's face. He wasn't the supposed truck thief. "No, I *know*."

"Okay, then why don't you ask your cousin if she can flex her political muscle to find out the name of the truck's owner?"

Why hadn't she thought of that? Her cousin Caroline Brennan was the chief aide to Edwina Funk, one of their state's senators. If anyone could get her a name, Caroline could. Laura called her immediately.

"It wouldn't be as easy as you think," Caroline said. "The police wouldn't withhold information without good reason. Let it go and leave them to do their job."

"Seriously? You won't even try to help me? All I'm asking for is a name."

"Yeah, and I know you. You'll do something with that name. Maybe something foolish."

"Wow, thanks for the vote of confidence." Laura floundered for a way to convince Caroline to change her mind. Admittedly they hadn't been all that close since Caroline had moved to Pittsburgh and taken the senator's aide job, but growing up they'd been inseparable and insatiably curious. Their grandmother used to call them the Bobbsey Twins from an old mystery series their mothers had read. And people had thought they *were* twins too, because they were so similar.

"I'm sorry I can't help you," Caroline said. "I really am."

Garrett picked up the *Gray's Anatomy* textbook from his uncle's desk to shelve it on the bookcase. Noticing his uncle had used a receipt as a bookmark, Garrett turned to the page. It depicted the circulatory system. A name was scribbled on the top of the receipt followed by a question mark, but unfortunately his uncle's handwriting was as cryptic as any stereotypical doctor's.

Leaving the book open on his desk, Garrett took the bookmark to his aunt. "Can you decipher this word?"

Jenny put on her reading glasses. "'Herb.'"

"Do you know why he might have written this?"

"Could be that he wanted to find an herb that would help a condition. The past few years he'd started to give more credence to the value of herbs, not necessarily as remedies but in supporting good health." She flipped over the receipt. "That's strange."

"What is?"

"This is a receipt for photocopies at the town's library," Jenny answered. "It's dated a couple of days before he died."

"Any idea what he might have copied?"

"No, I haven't seen any copies around here, and I don't recall him bringing any home. Why would he go there to make photocopies when we have a perfectly good photocopier here?"

"Good question." Garrett reclaimed the receipt. "I'll go to the library and see what I can dig up."

He'd been through his uncle's entire office. While there'd been the odd photocopied page here and there, none had stood out as significant. Maybe this receipt wasn't either. But between the attack on Laura at the cemetery and now the two break-ins, he wasn't willing to discount the possibility the incidents were connected to information his uncle had.

A few minutes later, Garrett strode into the library, which was housed in a century-old home.

"Dr. Simons, to what do we owe this pleasure?" Beth asked from the circulation desk.

"I was hoping you could help me." He scanned the adjoining rooms to see if curious ears might be nearby. Not spotting anyone, he joined Beth at the desk and showed her the receipt. "A couple of days before he died, my uncle made photocopies here. Would you happen to know what he copied?"

"I'm not sure. Every few days he'd stop by about something different."

"Like what?"

"Oh, all kinds of things," Beth said. "One was for records of aerial spraying of pesticides in this area. Another of rainfall records. He also went through the newspaper archives. I think he said he was looking for any mention of issues with the water treatment plant, chemical spills, things like that."

"Did he mention why he was doing it?"

"He had several patients exhibiting similar symptoms he couldn't explain. They were of diverse ages and occupations. The common denominator was that they all lived south of town."

"Had he considered Lyme disease?" In Garrett's experience, it was the most misdiagnosed ailment these days, given the magnitude of symptoms it could trigger.

"I asked the same thing. He said it was the first thing he tested for."

"I appreciate your help." Garrett lowered his voice. "Has anyone else been asking about Doc's research?"

"Not that I'm aware of," Beth said, clear suspicion in her tone.

"Good. Please let me know if anyone does ask."

"Of course. Do you think it has something to do with his death? That maybe it wasn't an accident?"

"I'm not sure what to think, but for now let's keep it quiet."

On Friday nights, Laura helped out with the church's youth group. Tonight was their annual baseball game against Calvary Community's team. Laura was the third base coach, but so far, she hadn't had a chance to coach many players, and they were already halfway through the game. It didn't help that they were missing their best batter, Matt Stephenson.

He'd said he had to work late at his summer job, lifeguarding at the community center pool, but Laura suspected there was more to it than that. He could've asked for the time off, as he had last year. But since Doc's death, it seemed to her Matt's job had become a convenient excuse to miss their weekly youth group gatherings.

She wasn't sure if it was shame or self-pity or if the others had razzed him for his role in Doc's accident. She hoped it wasn't the latter.

The slam of a car door drew her attention to the street. A green Mustang with a fresh paint job gleamed in the sun.

Matt rounded the vehicle and jogged over to her. "Is it too late for me to play a few innings?"

"Your timing is perfect." Laura motioned to Bill, who'd been organizing the batters. "Hey, Matt's here."

His fellow players cheered, and their opponents groaned. Everyone knew Matt was one of the few players who could readily hit a home run.

Catching Bill's attention, Laura brushed her thumb up her cheek, their signal to suggest he have the next batter bunt.

Bill nodded and intercepted Chloe after she left the bench.

At the plate, Chloe took a few practice swings as if she had every intention of knocking the ball out of the field, but the instant the pitcher released the ball, she pulled up on the bat and tipped the ball mere feet in front of her.

"Run!" Laura jumped up and down, trying to light a fire under their base runners.

The bases were loaded when Matt came to bat.

"Show them what you've got!" Laura shouted encouragingly.

Matt let the first wild pitch fly by without attempting to hit it.

"Ball one," the ump called.

The second throw was another ball.

Their players started to taunt the pitcher that he was too scared to let Matt hit one. Four balls would allow them to bring one run in, but they needed at least two to tie the game.

The next pitch sailed right over the plate, and Matt popped it over left field.

Laura winced but circled her arm and yelled to her base runners, encouraging them to run. If the left fielder caught the fly ball, the inning was over anyway, so they had no reason to hesitate.

Her third base runner was so quick he passed home plate almost before the ball breezed by the left fielder's glove.

"Go, go, go!" Laura shouted as her second base runner rounded third. She continued to circle her arm as their third runner approached.

Matt made it all the way to her at third base before his ball returned to the infield.

"Great job," Laura praised.

Matt ducked his head, appearing a tad uneasy about enjoying the glory.

After the game, which they won, Matt headed straight to his car rather than joining the rest of the group for hot dogs and ice cream in the picnic area.

Laura caught up to him. "Aren't you going to stay for the food? After all, we have you to thank for the win."

"I should get home," Matt said. "I'm teaching a swimming class first thing in the morning."

"It isn't even dark yet."

He shrugged.

"Is this about what happened to Doc?" Laura asked.

Matt slapped his baseball glove against his thigh and stared up at the sky, blinking hard. "If I hadn't let that guy goad me into racing him, Doc would still be alive."

"You don't know that." Laura had heard the driver rev the engine of the souped-up pickup. The noise had snagged her attention to the intersection where Matt was stopped for the red light in the lane beside the truck. She'd seen them exchange glances and knew what was coming. "You slowed down as soon as Doc came out of the store. I was there and saw you. Remember?"

"Yeah, but if I hadn't jumped on the gas the second the light changed, the other guy wouldn't have been watching me instead of the street," Matt argued. "If I'd really looked at the other driver, or I hadn't crashed into that mailbox and hit my head and blacked out, I might have been able to help the cops identify him."

Laura knew from experience that she wouldn't be able to talk him out of his guilty feelings, and maybe she wasn't supposed to. Maybe God had some giant lesson He wanted Matt to learn from all of this, besides the knowledge that it was never a good idea to street race. But she could at least reassure him that she understood what he was feeling. "If you ever want to talk about it, I'm here for you, okay?"

He nodded.

Laura could tell that he was never going to take her up on the offer, so she tried a different approach. "I went through a similar thing when my dad was killed."

That got his attention. "Your dad was killed?"

"Yeah, I was about your age. He fought back against a carjacker."

"I didn't know that."

Laura dipped her head and drew in a deep breath. "For a long time, I blamed myself."

The events of that night flashed through her mind—Dad telling her and Mom to wait while he fetched the car, the car squealing past them out of the parking garage, the passenger side door opening and her father's body flying out. Racing to him as he lay on the pavement, fighting for breath.

She swallowed hard, trying to contain her emotions. "I figured if I hadn't been so eager to see the hockey game in Pittsburgh, we wouldn't have been anywhere near the parking garage the night the carjacker picked our car to steal."

"How'd you get over it?" Matt asked.

Laura sighed, realizing that part of her probably never really had. She'd kept busy, like Matt seemed to be doing. For her that had meant working at the diner ever since, where memories of Dad hovered in every order she took, every cup of coffee she poured, every table she wiped clean. Memories she'd done her best to honor.

"Time helps." Her voice cracked. "So did knowing my dad wouldn't want me to live a life of what-ifs." Doc had impressed that truth on her the first day they'd reopened the diner after the funeral. He'd found her out back, crying behind the dumpster. "You know what I mean?"

"Yeah, I think I do. Thanks."

Laura clapped his shoulder. "Anytime. I mean that."

Matt still chose to head home.

Shutting off the memories and regaining her game face, Laura rejoined the group and indulged in an ice-cream cone.

But as she walked home later, her heart still felt heavy. Maybe partly from her concern for Matt. And partly from mulling over her conversation with the lieutenant.

At the sight of her cousin's car parked on the street in front of her house, Laura picked up her pace. With any luck, Caroline had changed her mind about helping.

As Laura drew closer, she spotted lights on inside her house. Apparently, her cousin had found the spare key. Laura reached into her pocket for her cell phone to see if she'd missed a call, but she remembered she'd left her phone at home when she decided to walk to the park. She jogged past the last few houses to her front door, pushed it open, and called Caroline's name.

No response. The only sound was the slap of the back screen door reverberating through the house.

"Caroline?" Laura repeated, assuming she'd been in the backyard the first time she called.

Again, no response.

Laura spotted a shadow move in the hall outside the kitchen. "Aren't we a little old to play hide-and-seek?" she cajoled. She headed toward the kitchen.

Something hard whacked her on the back of the head, knocking her to the floor. She tumbled onto her back and tried to focus on the blurry figure above her. She caught a glimpse of an inked design—a tattoo?—on her attacker's wrist before her vision went black.

Garrett pulled into his driveway after collecting his mother at the bus depot. "I wish you would've given me a few days to at least get the guest room set up for you. I'm afraid the best I can give you tonight is an air mattress."

"I don't mind. It'll be like our summer camping trips." His mom had always been game for anything. Having been a nurse before she retired last year, she was used to seeing people at their worst.

He opened the passenger door for her, then grabbed her suitcases from the trunk and carried them inside. "Go ahead and take a tour while I grab the groceries."

When Garrett returned to his car, he noticed Laura's front door ajar. The living room light spilled onto the porch. He was surprised she'd left it open without a screen door. It was a beautiful evening, but the mosquitoes were out in full force. He hefted his groceries from the back and paused, waiting to see if she returned to close it.

There was no sign of movement in the yard or the house.

He crossed the lawn between their yards and called to her. Hearing a groan, he abandoned his groceries and dashed to the front porch. He wavered only a moment on the threshold before rushing inside. He found her sprawled semiconscious in the hallway outside the kitchen. "Laura, can you hear me?"

Her eyes fluttered open.

"What happened?" Garrett asked.

"I-I'm not sure."

Garrett pulled a penlight from his pocket. Her pupils were equal and reactive. He held up two fingers. "How many fingers can you see?"

"Two."

"Good." He curled his fingers around her slim wrist and felt for her pulse. It was galloping. His own wasn't far behind. "Any idea how long you were out?"

Laura rubbed the back of her head. "I think something fell on me, but I can't imagine what."

Garrett spotted a heavy wooden rolling pin against the wall. "Did you see an intruder?" He eased her onto her side to examine the bump she'd incurred.

Gasping, she moved into a seated position, then winced, probably experiencing a throb of pain from the sudden movement. "I thought my cousin Caroline was here. I saw her car outside, and the front door was unlocked, the lights on. But she didn't answer me when I came in."

"Garrett, are you here?" his mom called from the front door.

"Back here," he said.

His mom joined them, sized up the situation, and pulled out her cell phone. "I'll call the police. Does she need an ambulance?"

"No, I don't think she needs to go to the hospital," Garrett said, then turned to Laura. "Do you have an ice pack?"

She nodded and pointed to the freezer.

He retrieved the pack. "Hold this against the back of your head. Let's get you up and seated on the sofa."

Laura swayed as she stood.

Garrett curled his arm around her waist to steady her. "Feeling dizzy?"

"I'm okay," she whispered. "Where's Caroline?"

Garrett's mom scanned the other rooms. "No one else is here."

Garrett introduced her to Laura. "My mom will be visiting me for a week or so."

"What does Caroline drive?" his mom asked Laura.

"A cherry-red 1976 Firebird," Laura said. "It's parked across the street."

Mom pushed the sheer curtain aside and looked out the window. "Not anymore, I'm afraid."

The mixture of disappointment and confusion on Laura's face worried Garrett. If her cousin had been here, why would she leave Laura defenseless? Or was she the one who'd taken the rolling pin to Laura's head?

Lieutenant Reynolds—the same officer who'd come by the day before—arrived a few minutes later.

Laura recounted what had happened, at least as much as she knew.

"Are you sure your cousin was inside?" Reynolds asked. "Could you have mistaken someone else's car for hers?"

"A Firebird of that vintage is pretty rare."

"But surely your cousin wouldn't have abandoned you to an intruder," Garrett countered.

"Maybe when I heard the back door, it was Caroline running out, not in, and she didn't realize I'd come home," Laura suggested.

"More likely the kids who burgled your diner decided to have a go at your house and panicked when you got home," Lieutenant Reynolds said. "Is anything missing?"

"I don't know." Laura snagged her cell phone from the end table next to the sofa.

"Who are you calling?" Reynolds demanded.

Laura bristled at the lieutenant's sharp tone.

Garrett felt a similar response in himself. Why was the man so abrupt?

"My cousin. It's the quickest way to learn which of us is right." Laura dialed Caroline's number, and a phone rang elsewhere in the house.

"It's coming from the room on the end," Garrett's mom called from the hall.

"Stay here." The lieutenant breezed past her, his palm resting on the butt of his gun in his holster.

Realizing Laura was holding her breath, her imagination no doubt running wild, Garrett squeezed her hand and was heartened by her reciprocation.

Lieutenant Reynolds rejoined them, unapologetic, a purple cell phone in his hand. "Looks like you were right about your cousin being here. Your burglar must've scared her off."

Garrett's mom appeared disturbed by the lieutenant's explanation. "If that was the case, she would've called by now to check on Laura."

The lieutenant wagged the cell phone. "No phone, remember?"

"She could've stopped at any local business and asked to borrow a phone," his mom said.

Reynolds shook his head. "No one memorizes phone numbers these days, not with the convenience of contact lists."

"She could have found the number in a phone book or gotten it from the operator," his mom reasoned.

"Or she could've been so preoccupied with trying to get away that it didn't occur to her to call," the lieutenant said, sounding irritated. "Like Laura said, her cousin never responded to her name, so she might not have realized Laura was home yet."

"Then she'd call the police to report the break-in," Garrett's mom insisted. "You've got to see something doesn't add up."

Garrett nodded. "That's a good point. Perhaps the intruder caught up to Caroline at her car and forced her to drive somewhere at gunpoint. You should issue a BOLO for the vehicle."

Laura shuddered, and Garrett instantly regretted voicing the theory.

"I can issue a BOLO," the lieutenant agreed. He asked Laura to see if anything was taken while he did so.

Garrett accompanied her.

"He must not have had time to ransack the drawers like he did at my office in the diner," Laura said, her voice shaky. "Do you think that was his intention?"

Garrett's chest squeezed at the anxiety she radiated. "What do you mean?"

"What if he came to grab me, like the guy at the cemetery, and mistook Caroline for me? Everyone always said we could be twins." She started to hyperventilate.

Garrett urged her to sit on the edge of her bed and take slow, deep breaths. "Let's not borrow trouble. Hopefully the police will locate her safe and sound. Or she'll stop and call you."

Garrett's mom stuck her head into the bedroom. "Laura should stay with us until the intruders are caught."

"Good idea," Garrett said.

"I couldn't impose," Laura protested. "You're scarcely moved in."

"Nonsense," his mom said. "His furniture arrives tomorrow. We can rough it for one night."

"I would feel safer," Laura admitted.

"It's settled then," Garrett declared. "Pack yourself an overnight bag."

Laura reported to the lieutenant that nothing appeared to be missing.

He dusted the front doorknob and the abandoned rolling pin for prints. "I'll let you know if these bring up any hits, but don't hold your breath. If we locate your cousin, I'll have her call you."

Garrett and his mom helped Laura gather what she'd need for the night and then escorted her back to his house.

A neighborhood cat sat on the lawn next to his abandoned groceries, cleaning his front paw.

"No!" Garrett raced toward the bags, scaring him off. He held up an empty package. "He ate our salmon."

His mom chuckled. "I feel like pizza anyway. Don't you, Laura?"

"That sounds kind of nice."

Garrett salvaged the rest of the groceries. "Okay, pizza it is."

He had hoped taking on his uncle's practice in this picturesque town would be the escape he needed after the mortar attack that left him battling PTSD, but everywhere he turned he encountered bandits—if not two-legged ones, then four-legged ones. He supposed he should be grateful he hadn't had an episode at the sight of Laura lying unconscious in the hallway. Hopefully he wouldn't relive it in his dreams tonight. If she woke to the sound of him battling demons in his sleep from another room, who knew how she'd react? She certainly wouldn't feel any safer under his roof.

Excusing herself, Laura disappeared into the bathroom to freshen up.

"She seems nice," his mom said in a pointed tone.

Garrett laughed. He'd learned years ago it was the best response. The last thing he wanted to do was encourage her. Not that he didn't like Laura. Truth be told, he'd felt drawn to her from the first time he met her and learned how she'd run to Uncle Richard's aid in his last moments. Then there was the overwhelming protectiveness he'd felt toward her after the incident in the cemetery. That had come out of nowhere, and he was still trying to figure it out.

Maybe it was another side effect of the PTSD—ensuring no one ever got hurt again on his watch.

Laura dutifully swallowed the acetaminophen Garrett gave her for her pounding head and tried to relax in his beanbag chair while he and his mom, Nancy, blew up air mattresses for them. She also tried to ignore the way her heart fluttered every time she met his eyes. When he'd so sweetly held her hand at her house, she'd hung on to it like a lifeline. The man must think she was helpless or a magnet for trouble. Not that it should matter to her what he thought.

Pressing her fingertips to her throbbing head, she tried harder to relax. She shuddered to think what state she'd be in if he hadn't come to her assistance. She supposed soldiers were trained to be that way. But his gaze on her when she'd come to hadn't felt like a soldier's—or a doctor's for that matter.

In fact, no one had looked at her like that since her high school sweetheart.

Laura let her mind wander back to the carefree summer she and Mel had enjoyed before her dad's death. She'd thought they'd always be together. Then after Dad died and they started talking about life after school, it had all fallen apart.

She shut down the thought and dug her phone out of her purse. The police still hadn't found Caroline's car, so Laura started calling every friend and relative she could think of who might know where Caroline was.

At some point, Garrett and Nancy joined her, chatting quietly with each other as she made her calls.

Eventually Garrett closed the distance between them and gently took the phone from her hand.

"What are you doing?" Laura asked.

"It's late. You should sleep. Doctor's orders."

Emotions flared at his bossiness, but she had to admit that she was exhausted. After saying good night to Garrett and his mom and repeating her thanks for their hospitality, she retreated to the room they'd given her. A small lamp sat beside the air mattress, which was layered with cozy blankets. She lay on the bed for a long time, waiting for sleep to overtake her. All she could hear were the distant revs of car engines and the mournful yowls of neighborhood cats.

After a fitful night's sleep, Laura awoke to the smell of sizzling bacon. Who was cooking in her house? She sprang to a sitting position and did a double take at the bare walls surrounding her. Not her house. It took her another couple of seconds to overcome her disorientation and remember she'd spent the night at Garrett's.

Memories of why quickly followed, and with them came a bone-rattling shudder.

Shaking off the feeling as best she could, she slipped into the bathroom and dressed, then plodded down the hall to the kitchen, where Nancy was setting out two plates with bacon and eggs and toast at the breakfast bar.

"Oh no!" Laura exclaimed when she saw the clock on the stove. "I should've been at the diner an hour ago."

"Not to worry," Nancy assured her. "Garrett spoke to your cook first thing this morning."

"He did?" Laura didn't know whether to be touched by his thoughtfulness or unnerved by the fact that he'd taken it upon himself to call without consulting her first.

"Your cook said your part-timer was scheduled to be in and could handle it," Nancy continued.

"Right, I forgot it was Saturday." Laura willed herself to calm.

"Now sit down and eat before your breakfast gets cold," Nancy urged. "Garrett will be back in a minute. He's on the phone with the police station."

Laura took a seat at the table.

Nancy sat down across from her. As she sipped her coffee, she eyed Laura over the rim of her mug. "So, tell me about yourself."

"Not much to tell. I'm thirty-two. I've lived next door all my life. My mom lived with me until she decided to move in with her sister-in-law six years ago. I took over the diner from her and have been running it ever since."

"You have any siblings?"

"No, I'm an only child. My dad passed when I was in high school."

"I'm sorry."

"It was a long time ago." Laura filled her mouth with food to spare her from having to share anything more about herself.

"Garrett says you enjoy gardening."

Laura nodded, oddly touched that he'd mentioned that to his mother.

Nancy motioned to the vase of flowers Laura had cut for him, displayed prominently in the center of the counter. "I couldn't help but notice the lovely bouquet."

Laura offered a small smile between bites.

"Garrett used to pick me bouquets of wildflowers when he was a boy. He's always been thoughtful that way. He's handy around the house too. Some people are surprised by that, him being a doctor and with all the studying that entailed."

Getting the sense that Nancy was trying to convince Laura of her son's merits, Laura smothered a giggle. Nancy and Beth would get along like two peas in a pod.

"I'd never imagined in a million years he'd join the army," Nancy went on. "But it was important to him to not accumulate debt in the pursuit of his degree, and he wanted to serve his country. I'm so proud of him."

"As you should be," Laura agreed.

Garrett joined them in the kitchen. If he'd overheard his mother touting his good qualities, he didn't let on. "I'm afraid I have discouraging news. There have still been no sightings of Caroline or her car. Her condo superintendent reports that she isn't there. The police left a message at the senator's office to have her call them if she comes in, but since it's Saturday, no one will likely get the message until Monday."

Laura's insides churned, and she pushed away what was left of the delicious breakfast Nancy had made for her. If Caroline was okay, she would've called by now. Unless she didn't know Laura knew she'd stopped by. But then, at the very least, she would've called the police about the intruder.

Which could only mean the bad guys had Caroline.

No matter how Laura analyzed it, she kept coming to the same conclusion. And if the police couldn't find Caroline, it was up to her.

Rising, Laura thanked Nancy for breakfast and Garrett for his hospitality. "I need to go home and shower, then at least put in an appearance at the diner."

"Are you sure you feel up to it?" Nancy asked, then glanced at Garrett as if seeking his opinion.

"It might help to stay occupied," he countered.

Laura nodded. Not that she would have been dissuaded if he had nixed the idea.

Garrett walked her home to make sure it was safe and clear of invaders.

Laura searched for any clues her assailant might've left and found nothing.

As she got ready for work, a disturbing thought returned. *Had* the kidnapper mistaken Caroline for Laura? He wouldn't expect to see Laura at the diner. If he believed he already had Laura, he wouldn't be looking for her there. What if he heard through the grapevine it was business as usual at the diner? That Laura hadn't mysteriously disappeared?

He'd realize his mistake in nabbing Caroline. Then what?

Laura frowned. Surely if the guy were after her, it would be good for him to realize he had the wrong woman. Then he'd let Caroline go.

But what would that mean for Laura?

Garrett peered out his side window toward Laura's house for the umpteenth time since she'd left. His gut told him the rash of break-ins and attacks had to be connected. Clearly someone was searching for something. Why couldn't Lieutenant Reynolds see that?

His mother's voice broke into his thoughts. "If you want to help Laura, why don't you ask your old school friend who works for the state police to check out your uncle's case file? He should be able to tell you who owns the supposedly stolen truck and give you some insight into anything suspicious going on there."

"Great idea," Garrett said.

His mom chuckled. "I do have them from time to time."

He kissed her cheek and then pulled up Joel Layton's number. After Garrett explained the situation, Joel promised to get back to him with whatever he could find.

"I like Laura," his mom said the moment Garrett disconnected with Joel.

"Don't get any ideas," he warned, knowing how eager she was to see him happily married. "I'm in no condition to think about starting a relationship."

She frowned. "Still having the nightmares?"

"You didn't hear me last night?" Garrett hadn't had one that bad since the night of Uncle Richard's funeral and the attack on Laura at the cemetery.

Movement outside caught his attention. "She's leaving."

His mom smiled. "Go."

Fighting the urge to do exactly that, he said, "I can't leave you here alone. What if last night's prowler comes back?"

"Not likely when the movers are due in a few minutes."

Yeah, and those guys would be built like tanks. "You're sure you don't mind?"

"Of course not." She laughed. "This way I can tell them to put the furniture wherever I like."

Garrett wavered.

"You know I love to decorate," his mom said. "I'll take care of things here."

He kissed her cheek. "You're the best." He slid his laptop into his satchel, then hurried out. Catching up to Laura, he asked, "Mind if I walk with you?"

She squinted at him somewhat warily. "You're walking to town?"

Garrett patted the satchel he'd slung over his shoulder, wishing he could alleviate the fears that were clearly eating at her. "I thought I'd work on my laptop at the diner."

"But your mom just fed you an amazing breakfast not more than an hour ago."

"Ah, but her coffee doesn't hold a candle to yours."

Laura shook her head. "You don't have to play bodyguard. You've seen the size of my cook, right? He wouldn't let anyone mess with me."

"Glad to hear it. But the fact is I need to review my uncle's patient files, and I can do it over coffee at the diner more easily than in my unfurnished office at home." Not to mention that he wouldn't be able to concentrate if he stayed home. He'd be too worried that the creep who'd hit her would come back.

"What about your mom?" she asked, apparently self-conscious about his concern.

"She'll delight in arranging my kitchen cupboards and furniture however she thinks best, without me there to interfere."

Laura laughed—a sound that seemed to finally dispel the cloud she'd been walking under. "I like your mom."

"I'm told the feeling is mutual."

She gained a little spring in her step at that tidbit of information. "I have to stop by the library to return the novel I've finished."

Garrett glanced at the title. "A mystery?"

"More of a thriller." Laura shuddered. "It'll be a long while before I want to read another one. These days, the stories are getting a little too close to real life."

"I hear you. If you want to escape reality, I'm told romances are a good choice."

That earned him another laugh. "Spoken like a true man."

He shrugged. Between medical school and army life, he hadn't had many opportunities to romance a woman. Truth be told, he'd always been a little intimidated about striking up a conversation, let alone asking a woman out, but bantering with Laura felt effortless.

The library was only a block out of their way.

When they arrived, Laura slipped the book through the return slot on the outside of the building. "Thank you."

"For what?"

"For making me forget my worries for a few minutes. For caring. For being here."

Her brown eyes turned a little watery, revealing shades and highlights he'd never seen in a woman's eyes before. And as a doctor, he'd observed a lot of eyes. Realizing he was staring, he smiled.

"I didn't tell you that when I returned to my house this morning, I noticed there was a tea bag I didn't put there sitting in a dry teacup and the kettle was next to the sink. I phoned Lieutenant

Reynolds to tell him, since it's further proof Caroline intended to stay for a visit."

"I'd agree with that. What did he say?"

Laura grimaced. "He assured me they're doing all they can to locate her."

"You don't sound as if you believe him."

"I'd like to see a massive search for Caroline and her picture plastered all over the news. But I'm sure the press would have a field day with the fact that a senator's aide has gone missing."

"Your cousin is a senator's aide?"

"Yes."

Garrett realized that could be a game changer. Maybe this intruder wasn't connected to the other burglaries. "So, it's possible your cousin's abductor—if she was abducted—is someone with nothing to do with you."

"I don't think so. I didn't even know she was coming to visit." Laura sucked in a deep breath and exhaled on a shaky sigh. "I'm more afraid her kidnapper will discover she's not who he thinks she is and decide she's a liability."

Laura almost wished she hadn't mentioned her call to the lieutenant to Garrett. For a few brief minutes walking with Garrett, she'd managed to escape the worries squeezing her chest.

When they reached the diner, Garrett held the door open for her.

Her heart actually hiccuped at the chivalrous gesture. She clearly needed to get out more. A passing truck backfired, making her jump.

Garrett instantly shifted his position, shielding her from the street. "A little skittish today, are we?" Old Mr. Horton chuckled from where he was sweeping the walk in front of his secondhand shop next door.

Garrett made no apology as he urged Laura inside with a gentle press to the small of her back that made her feel warm and safe.

Laura relaxed to see the diner full of her regulars. She greeted her cook and teenage waitress, then poured Garrett a cup of coffee.

After ensuring the waitress was adequately handling the morning rush, Laura retreated to her office to repeat all the phone calls she'd made the night before—the senator's office, mutual friends, Caroline's friend Anita from the newspaper where she used to work. The answers were the same—no one had seen Caroline or heard from her.

Bracing herself, Laura phoned her mother and Aunt Liz, her father's sister. She hated to worry the women with another call, but it had to be done. Last night she'd talked to her aunt because her mother hadn't been home. Laura had managed to casually ask Liz if either had heard from Caroline, without letting on there was any need for concern. But Laura feared her mother and Liz were astute enough to see through her if she tried that a second time.

Mom answered the phone. "I'm glad you called again, since I missed you last night."

"What are you and Liz up to today?" Laura figured that was a safe question. Her mother tended to share their goings-on in minute detail, which meant if Caroline had called or dropped by, Mom would say so.

Mom was relating details of the Waldorf salad she'd made for an afternoon picnic at their seniors' club when Beth burst into the office.

Laura took one look at Beth's flushed face and said to her mom, "Sorry, but I've got to go. I'm needed here." She hung up.

Garrett had trailed Beth to the office.

Beth uncharacteristically grabbed the door and shut him out, saying, "Girl stuff."

Laura sprang to her feet. "What's going on?"

"Caroline left you a note," Beth blurted.

"What?" Laura had texted Beth last night to tell her what happened at the house, but she couldn't imagine Caroline contacting Beth.

Beth opened the book she'd brought with her, the novel Laura had just returned, and removed a piece of paper.

Laura snatched it from her. "I never put that in there." She read the note aloud. "'I wanted to talk to you in person, but I forgot you have youth group Friday nights. The wrong—'" An abrupt line followed the word, as if she'd been startled maybe, and then the writing became choppy. "'They've found me. Don't trust anyone. I'll be in touch.'" Her hand trembled. "Garrett was right. The intruder *was* after Caroline, not me."

"Who do you think found her?" Beth asked.

"I have no idea. Maybe someone who's involved with whatever she's working on for the senator. But I'm not sure if I should ask Senator Funk—if I even knew how to contact her on a weekend."

"Any idea what Caroline came to town to tell you?"

"None. I'd asked her earlier in the day to find out who owned the truck that killed Doc. But she told me no. When I first saw her car, I thought maybe she'd changed her mind." Laura shook her head. "What do I do now? I can't show this to the police. Not when Caroline warned me not to trust anyone."

"You know that doesn't apply to me, right?" Beth said.

"Of course. But what about Garrett?" Laura's insides twisted. She wanted to tell him. He'd already saved her twice. And what if the guy came back? After Lieutenant Reynolds's reaction to her conclusions about Doc's killer, she couldn't rely on the police to protect her.

"As much as I hate to say it," Beth said, "Garrett seems to show up a little too conveniently every time you're in trouble."

"Seriously?" Laura asked. Beth was the last person she would've expected to dissuade her from anything that might strengthen her relationship with a man. But then again, Laura probably wasn't seeing him objectively. The heroine in the book had been duped by a would-be hero too.

"Caroline said don't trust anyone," Beth said.

Swallowing hard, Laura nodded. What if Garrett was exactly who Caroline had meant?

Garrett had switched tables to one that allowed him an unobstructed view of Laura's office door. When she walked her friend out, much paler than before Beth arrived, he shut his laptop and returned it to his satchel.

Laura poured herself a coffee with more concentration than the task really required, then turned back toward her office.

Grabbing his bag, Garrett intercepted her. "What's going on?"

Laura's wary look left him crushed.

He wondered what Beth had said to her.

She backed toward her office, muttering something about calls she needed to make. Her cell phone rang, and she glanced at the screen. "It's a friend of Caroline's who works at a newspaper. I left her a voice mail last night."

Garrett trailed Laura into her office, and this time he didn't give her the chance to shut him out. "Can you put the call on speaker—" He didn't bother finishing his request, since the caller spoke so loudly, he didn't need it on speaker.

"Caroline called me Friday to ask about an article I did on Pennsylvania's biggest polluters," the friend said. "I think it was for a report she had to prepare for the senator."

"Did she mention anything else going on with her?" Laura fished.

"Oh, you mean about her breaking up with her boyfriend— Dwayne Connor? He clearly didn't take it very well."

Laura appeared surprised by the news. Apparently, she and her cousin weren't as close as Garrett had assumed.

"How do you mean?" Laura asked.

"You know, calling her all the time, showing up at her work and her house and even at her events with the senator. He always struck me as a bit of a stalker type. That probably explains why she's gone incognito on you."

Laura tensed.

Garrett pressed his back to the office door and stayed the impulse to reach out to her.

"Caroline probably decided to get away for the weekend," the friend went on, "with no phones or way for her ex to contact her."

"You wouldn't happen to have his address or phone number, would you?" Laura asked.

"No, sorry. And you might not see anything about him online either. I doubt he had a landline—so many people don't these days—and Caroline said he had a real phobia about being on social media and stuff."

"Was this the guy with dark hair and glasses?" Laura probed.

"I never saw him in glasses, and his hair was blond. You must be thinking of the guy she dated before Dwayne."

"Oh, right," Laura said. "Dwayne's the tall, lanky guy."

"Not all that tall. Under six feet and muscular."

"I'm barely over five feet, so it doesn't take much for a guy to be tall as far as I'm concerned."

The woman laughed. "I hear you. Sorry I couldn't be of more help."

"Actually, this has been very helpful," Laura said. "Thank you."

The instant she disconnected the call, Garrett asked, "Do you think your cousin could be running from this Dwayne guy?"

Laura hesitated. "Maybe."

"But you think the guy who hit you had dark hair and glasses?"

"I'm not sure." Laura set her cell phone on her desk and shuffled a few of the pages lying there, almost as if she were afraid to make eye contact. "I only caught a glimpse of him before I went unconscious. It was more like a silhouette."

"We should call the police. They have the resources to track down Dwayne's address. He must have a driver's license."

Laura winced and shook her head. "Caroline wouldn't want me to do that."

"What are you talking about? This morning you were frustrated the police weren't doing enough, but now you don't want to involve them when they could be of real use?"

Laura sank into her chair and clutched her head. "I need time to think."

Garrett approached the desk and tapped the purple cell phone lying on top. "Is that your cousin's?"

Laura lowered her hands from her face enough to peek at what he was talking about. "Yes."

"So Dwayne's phone number is bound to be in there."

Laura slapped her hand on the desk. "Undoubtedly. But I don't know her password."

Garrett didn't take her outburst personally. Her frustration was understandable. "Mind if I take a crack at it?"

"Knock yourself out."

Laura regretted her response the instant it left her lips. Caroline had warned her not to trust anyone, and here Laura had given Caroline's phone to Garrett. Then again, the chances of him guessing the password were slim to none. Truth be told, she wasn't sure she'd encountered Dwayne in her house last night. Not that she wanted to admit it to Garrett.

Well, she did. She wanted to talk to him about everything, but like Beth had said, Garrett was showing up to her aid awfully conveniently. And now he seemed intent on insinuating himself into her business. Laura wanted to believe it was because he cared, but who was she kidding? They barely knew each other. Besides, she hated to admit how out of touch she'd been with Caroline that she hadn't even known she was dating Dwayne.

Laura was pretty certain the guy who struck her last night wore glasses. Of course, they might've been sunglasses, and it could've been her vision closing in on her that made his hair look dark. Either way, this fretting was accomplishing nothing. She switched on her computer to conduct an Internet search on Dwayne Connor. With any luck, Caroline's friend was wrong about him not being online.

The search engine coughed up thirty-plus guys who shared the name in Pittsburgh alone. *Terrific.*

"Got it." Garrett passed Caroline's phone to Laura.

"Seriously? What was it?"

"'Snake.'"

"How in the world did you come up with that?"

"One of my colleagues got a Dear Jane letter while we were on a tour of duty." Garrett grinned. "She was so ticked she changed the password on her phone from her boyfriend's name to a much more colorful nickname."

"That sounds like Caroline." Laura scrolled through the contact list. "Dwayne isn't in here."

"Check the call log. Her friend said he'd been harassing her with calls."

"Good thinking." Laura tapped the screen a few times. "Oh,

here." She frowned at the nearly blank list. The lone call was from her own cell last night. "Caroline must've cleared the incoming call log recently."

"How about blocked numbers?" Garrett asked. "He's bound to be on it."

"Found it. But there are twenty-five numbers on it."

"Does she date a lot?"

"No, she's hardly a femme fatale. These are probably telemarketers. Quite a few of the numbers have area codes I don't recognize." Laura compared those on the list with local area codes to those of the Dwayne Connors she'd found online. "No matches here." She picked up the receiver of her landline. "I'll try some of her other contacts."

But before Laura could punch in the first number on the list, Caroline's phone died.

"No!" Laura dug through her desk drawers. "My phone charger is at home."

"Mine too. Sorry." Garrett scraped his hand over his clean-shaven jaw. "We could drive into Pittsburgh and explore your cousin's apartment."

Laura tensed. Why was he so eager to help her? She chided herself. Caroline couldn't have meant Garrett when she said not to trust anyone. How would he even know her cousin? He'd just gotten out of the army.

"What do you think?" Garrett asked.

"I appreciate the offer, but you must have a million things to do with preparing to take over Doc's practice. Besides, your mother is here to visit you."

He waved off her objections. "Mom planned to spend the afternoon and evening with Jenny, and I can't do much at the office until the replacement computers arrive."

"Don't you have furniture arriving today?"

"Already in. Mom texted me half an hour ago. Listen, I know you're concerned about your cousin, and I'm concerned about your well-being."

The warmth in his voice set off butterflies in Laura's stomach. She tried to ignore them. "Why are you concerned about me?"

"I'm a doctor. It's in my nature."

She raised her eyebrows.

"Okay, the truth is I'm concerned that your troubles are connected to my uncle."

Laura expelled a sigh. If she showed him the note Caroline left her, he might not think they were connected. Then again, if it was Caroline's boyfriend who had "found" her, that didn't involve his uncle either. But if it was her ex, why would Caroline warn her not to trust anyone? Wouldn't she have been more specific?

Laura couldn't imagine what Caroline needed to talk to her about that she couldn't have said over the phone—unless it had to do with Laura's call asking her to get the name of the truck's owner. Maybe she'd changed her mind about looking into it.

What if Garrett was being so friendly and protective to win her confidence and ensure she didn't cause problems for the person behind whatever was going on? *If* something was going on.

Except Dr. London was Garrett's uncle. Why would the bad guys steal all their office computers if Garrett was taking over the office and would have complete access to everything on them anyway? It didn't add up.

Maybe they would get answers at Caroline's apartment. It might be the only place they would. Laura had a key from the last time she'd visited and needed to get in while Caroline was at work.

"What do you say?" Garrett asked. "Shall we drive into Pittsburgh?"

"Give me a minute." Laura did a covert computer search on Garrett. He'd been his high school valedictorian, and he had earned an army commendation medal, a meritorious service medal, and two bronze stars. He didn't seem to have any skeletons in his closet. She pushed back from the desk. "Sure. Let's go."

Laura left the diner in her staff's capable hands. Since they had to walk back to Garrett's for his car, she picked up her cell phone charger and car inverter from her house. As she was leaving, she spotted her letter opener on her desk and tucked it into her purse in case she needed to defend herself.

Garrett ushered Laura to his car. She plugged Caroline's phone in to charge.

The drive to Pittsburgh seemed longer than usual. When the silence in the car became uncomfortable, Laura asked Garrett questions about army life. To her surprise, that actually made him equally quiet. She'd heard that soldiers and even cops tended to dislike discussing their experiences with civilians. She wasn't sure why, but she hoped it wasn't the reason Caroline had warned her not to trust anyone. Laura's insides churned. Caroline hadn't named Garrett specifically, but what if he was involved and Caroline hadn't known?

"Here we are," Garrett announced, parking outside Caroline's apartment building.

Key in hand, Laura fortified herself with a deep breath before climbing out of the car. "Her apartment is on the second floor."

"Let's take the stairs."

Laura didn't ask why. She wanted to think he preferred the exercise, but she had the uneasy feeling he was more concerned about being trapped by the enemy in an eight-by-eight space. She really needed to stop reading thrillers.

Garrett was in full soldier mode by the time they reached the door to the second floor. He motioned her to stay back as he opened it and scanned the hallway. "Okay, all clear."

"If you're trying to scare me, you're doing a good job."

He frowned. "Sorry. But we can't be too careful."

Laura pointed to the right. "Caroline's apartment is this way." She held out the key. "Do you want to do the honors?"

"You don't mind?"

"After that display, I think I'd be relieved."

"I'm sure there's nothing to worry about."

"Better safe than sorry." Laura pointed to 204. "That's the one."

Garrett knocked, and the door shifted. "It's open," he whispered. "Stay back." He pressed his back to the wall at the hinge side of the door, then slowly opened the door. "Caroline, are you home? I'm a friend of your cousin's."

No response.

Garrett pressed a finger to his lips, signaling Laura to stay quiet, then edged around the doorframe. His gasp sent a chill down Laura's back.

"What is it?" She craned her neck for a glimpse and clapped her hand over her mouth in horror.

Caroline's apartment had been ransacked.

After waiting for Garrett to confirm no one still lurked in her cousin's apartment, Laura picked up the books strewn across the floor.

Garrett whistled. "I'd say this nixes your theory that your intruder mistook Caroline for you. You probably shouldn't touch anything before the police get here."

"No, we can't call the police."

"Why? This pretty much proves someone is after your cousin—if he doesn't already have her."

Laura wasn't ready to explain why she couldn't go to the police with this. "Let's try to figure out what the intruder wanted first. Otherwise, they might not let us search, and I know my cousin better than any city cop."

Garrett stared at her for an uncomfortably long moment. "I guess it won't hurt. Lieutenant Reynolds likely alerted the Pittsburgh PD to the BOLO they issued for Caroline's car." He scanned the room. "Do you know where she kept her address book?"

Laura set the books she'd collected on the end table and righted one of the overturned drawers. "I imagine in one of these, if she had one. Why don't you see if you can get into the computer while I sort through this mess?"

Ten minutes later, Laura had the drawers back in place and refilled as best she could. "No sign of an address book and not so much as a sticky note, photo, or business card with Dwayne's name on it."

Garrett sprang from the wheeled desk chair and shoved it at the desk. "The intruder erased her hard drive."

"Are you sure? Could it just be some security feature that keeps it hidden from you?"

"No, it's been wiped."

"Maybe she did it herself before she left," Laura said. "If she knew someone was after something, she might've taken precautions."

"I think it's time to call the police."

"Wait. I haven't checked the bedroom yet. Caroline always used to keep a journal. Perhaps she still does." Laura led the way to the bedroom, where they found chaos that matched the rest of the apartment. The sheets had been torn off the bed, boxes pulled from the closet, clothes drawers rummaged through.

"I'll go through her jacket pockets for receipts or anything else that might be useful," Garrett said. "You try to find her journal."

Laura combed through the night table drawer and the items flung on the floor. Nothing. She lifted the mattress. Again nothing.

She backed up, then jumped when a floorboard squeaked beneath her foot. She bounced on it, recalling the same kind of squeaky floorboard Caroline had had in her childhood bedroom. Her pulse quickened. Laura dropped to her knees and ran her hands over the old pine board floor for a loose section. There was one under the edge of the bed frame. She worked her fingers into the gap and pried up the board. A leather journal rested beneath it. "Found it." She snatched the book and held it up for Garrett to see. "She had a hiding spot like this as a kid too."

Laura sat on the bed and leafed through the journal. "Nothing stands out as helpful. She mentions Dwayne a few times but nothing to indicate where he lives or works."

Garrett peered at the journal over her shoulder. "Although I could see a crazed ex trashing her place, wiping her hard drive might be a stretch. Does she mention anything she's doing for the senator that has her nervous?"

Laura thumbed through the most recent entries, but they were more than two weeks old. "She doesn't write about her work." She closed the journal and returned to the living room to take a second look at the books and papers she'd collected off the floor. There were only a few loose-leaf pages, all recipes printed off the Internet. "When Caroline was in college, she wrote everything longhand, then typed it, but there are no notebooks or scraps of paper with anything like that."

Laura went to the kitchen and peeked into the trash can. Empty.

Garrett shoved the chair away from the desk. "There's a bin under here." He pulled it out and removed a single crumpled piece of paper. "It says, 'What's PrimeCorp selling to the army?' Any idea what that's about?"

"Not a clue. You were in the army. Does it mean anything to you?"

He shook his head. "I assume it has to do with her work for the senator."

"But does it have anything to do with why she's missing?" Laura inspected the trash bin for herself. "There's a torn photo stuck to the bottom." She put the pieces together, and a picture of Caroline with a smiling guy at her side emerged.

"I'm guessing that's the ex," Garrett said. "Could he have been the guy who struck you?"

Like Caroline's friend had said, he had blond hair and didn't wear glasses. He had an average build, and in the picture, he didn't stand any taller than Caroline. But the sight of him didn't strike Laura as familiar. "I'm not sure," she hedged. She turned the photo pieces over, but nothing was written on the back.

The scrape of a key in the door lock made her jump.

Garrett swept his arm around her waist and tugged her behind the desk. "Stay down."

Her heart galloped. She wasn't sure if it was because of his touch or the thought of who might be trying to get in.

A man with a toolbox sauntered through the door.

"May I help you?" Garrett asked, standing.

"Who are you?" the man demanded. "What are you doing in Ms. Brennan's apartment?"

Laura peeked over the edge of the desk.

"You are home," the man said. "I'm sorry. I would have knocked."

Laura surged to her feet as what he said sank in. *Home.* He thought she was Caroline.

Garrett's scowl communicated that he wasn't happy she'd disobeyed his order to stay down.

"I didn't see your car outside, so I thought you'd already left for the day." The man gestured with his toolbox. "I came to fix the sink." His gaze drifted, taking in the state of the apartment, then zeroed in on Garrett. "Are you okay? Is this guy bothering you?"

Concluding the man was the building manager, Laura explained who she was and what they were doing and that the apartment had been broken into. As an afterthought, she realized Caroline would probably be annoyed she'd entrusted him with that much information.

"That's why the cop called about her?" the man asked. "I didn't check her apartment because her car wasn't in the parking lot."

"Did you see any strangers around the building in the last twenty-four hours or so?" Garrett asked.

"No." The man scraped his fingers through his hair, his face suddenly drawn. "And the other three tenants on this floor are away for the weekend."

"Anyone on the first floor who might've seen something?" Garrett persisted.

"Mr. Hillier, but he's not in right now. He left half an hour ago for his weekly golf game. Have you called the police?"

"They're aware of the trouble my cousin's been having," Laura jumped in, hoping the partial truth would satisfy him enough to not call now.

He seemed relieved by the fact. "It won't take long to fix the sink. You want me to do that now?"

Garrett shook his head ever so slightly.

Laura pretended she hadn't seen it. "You might as well."

After the man disappeared into the bathroom, Garrett said, "You sure that was a good idea?"

"I'd rather he fixes it while we're here," Laura said. "He might come back when we're gone and start nosing around. Although considering he has a key, I suppose there's nothing to stop him from doing that the moment we leave."

"We could take the photo you found to Caroline's friend at the newspaper to ask her if he's the ex," he suggested. "Do you think she'd be in the office on a Saturday?"

"I can call her and see."

Laura told herself Garrett was trying to be helpful, not trying to track Caroline for his own nefarious reasons, especially since Laura couldn't fathom what those reasons might be. Why would Caroline tell Laura not to trust anyone if it was Dwayne who'd caught up to her? Whoever she was worried about probably had something to do with her work for the senator.

But either way, if Dwayne was a creepy stalker as Caroline's friend had implied, he might've seen who else was following her.

Garrett had an uneasy feeling Laura wasn't telling him something. As they shared the elevator to the newspaper's fourth floor, she stared at the carpet. Ever since Beth's visit, Laura had been different. "Are you okay?"

She shot the briefest glance at him. "As fine as I can be with my cousin missing."

"We'll find her." He squeezed her shoulder.

She withdrew from his touch, and the reaction stung.

"Did I do something to upset you?" Garrett asked.

"No, I'm sorry. Reflex."

He knew that women who reacted that way to a man's touch usually suffered from a serious traumatic event. Was it the attack at her house? Or something else? She hadn't recoiled from him when he'd helped her to the sofa after she'd been attacked in her home.

"Coming?" Laura asked, standing in the hallway outside the elevator.

Garrett strode out and assessed the scene, reminding himself that he was here to keep her safe.

A petite redhead with a sharply cut bob flagged them to her desk. "You must be Caroline's cousin. You two look exactly alike," she said to Laura. "I'm Anita."

Laura thanked her for agreeing to see them and produced the taped-together photograph she'd retrieved from her cousin's trash. "Is this Dwayne?"

Anita laughed. "I figured she'd shred her pictures. Yes, that's him." She handed Laura a couple of printouts and tapped the top page. "After I talked to you, I remembered that Caroline mentioned this news article when she called."

Laura shifted her stance as she read, preventing Garrett from seeing it.

Was the action deliberate? He chided himself for reading too much into her body language. She was upset about her cousin's disappearance and likely wasn't even aware she'd shut him out.

A guy in casual attire passed by. From the sheaf of papers he was carrying, Garrett would have guessed that he was an employee, but he slowed and eyed the paper Laura pored over.

Garrett repositioned himself, and the guy moved on. From this vantage point, Garrett could glimpse the article's headline, something about PrimeCorp Manufacturing. That couldn't be a coincidence. Maybe he needed to reach out to his former commander and see what he could dig up on PrimeCorp's connection to the army.

"Are you familiar with this?" Laura asked Anita.

"Just what I read there. Caroline and I cowrote the article below it when she worked for us a few years ago. It's about polluters, so I thought she wanted to revisit it for something to do with the senator. But most of the article was about an industrial accident that killed a guy at one of PrimeCorp's plants. It might be why the recent headline caught her eye."

Garrett nodded. It could still have to do with the senator. She might've heard the company's name bandied about the senator's office in connection with government contracts.

Laura thanked Anita for her help.

Anita returned the photo, telling them the name of the restaurant where it had been taken. "You might ask for Dwayne's phone number there. They always ask for a phone number when you book a reservation."

Garrett entered the restaurant into the maps app on his phone. "It's ten minutes away." He turned to Laura. "Hungry?"

"Famished."

Garrett's spirits lightened at the enthusiasm in her voice.

The restaurant proved to be an upscale establishment—dimly lit, richly furnished, and tables set with linen napkins and crystal water goblets.

"Dwayne must've been serious about your cousin," Garrett said. In his circle, the only time a guy took a woman to a place like this was to propose.

"Or rich."

"Hmm." Garrett asked the hostess for a table.

"Do you have a reservation, sir?"

"No." Garrett couldn't believe she was serious. It was four o'clock, and the place was empty.

Still, the woman sniffed and made a point of checking the seating plan on her tablet screen.

"Do you keep records of past reservations?" Laura asked.

The hostess shook her head and snatched up a couple of menus. "Follow me, please." She led them to the table closest to the kitchen door.

Garrett glanced down at his wrinkled chinos and casual polo shirt. Clearly the woman didn't anticipate him being a repeat customer.

"We're trying to find a guy who brought my cousin here a month or two ago." Laura showed the hostess the photo. "Do you recognize him?"

The woman held out a chair for Laura. The hostess repeated the routine for Garrett and set a linen napkin on each of their laps before handing them menus.

"It's very important," Laura pressed. "She's disappeared, and we're hoping he might know where she is."

The hostess took the photo from Laura and studied it a moment before handing it back. "I'm sorry, but I don't recognize him."

"His name is Dwayne Connor," Laura said. "Would you have a record of his phone number if he made a reservation?"

"No, as I said," she repeated more tersely this time, "we don't keep records of past reservations. Your waitress will be with you shortly."

When the waitress finally appeared, Laura repeated her inquiry.

The young woman seemed much more eager to help than the hostess. When she didn't recognize the photo, she snapped a picture of it with her cell phone.

Laura snatched the photo. "What are you doing?"

"I'll show it around to the other staff to see if any of them recognize him," the waitress explained. "Can I get you something to drink?"

"I'll try one of your craft root beers," Laura said.

"Make that two," Garrett said.

After the woman left, Laura said, "You don't think she'll do something foolish, like post the photo to her social media account to ask if anyone knows him, do you?"

Garrett grimaced. "These days? Yeah, she might."

"I should've cut Caroline out of the picture." Laura stood and trailed the woman to the bar, where she was already showing the bartender the image on her phone.

He shook his head.

Laura spoke to her, and the woman nodded.

Laura was much calmer when she returned to their table. "She promised to delete the photo as soon as she's shown it to all the staff. Some don't come in for another hour."

Over a tossed salad and homemade pasta, Garrett asked Laura about her family.

"I'm an only child and so is Caroline, which is probably why we were as close as sisters growing up. My aunt and uncle used to live down the street from us until he got transferred when we were in ninth grade. After that Caroline and I talked on the phone a lot."

To his surprise, Laura didn't mention losing her father in high school, something he'd learned from his mother, who must've picked it up from his aunt. He understood too well not wanting to talk about loss, especially in a public place, so he decided not to ask about her dad. For now. But the decision didn't abate his curiosity about Laura, and as much as he didn't want to admit it, his interest went deeper than understanding the connection to his uncle's death.

The waitress delivered the bill to his side of the table.

"I'll pay for half," Laura said, digging into her purse.

"No, it's my treat," Garrett said. When she looked as if she'd put up a fight, he added, "I owe you one for that delicious lunch you brought my aunt and me yesterday."

She rolled her eyes but relented.

"Unfortunately, none of the staff recognized the guy in the photo," the waitress said. She made a point of letting Laura see her delete the photo from her phone.

Laura thanked her for trying.

"Before we go back to Hopeton, should we see if Caroline's first-floor neighbor is home and saw anything?" Garrett asked.

"Do you mind?"

"Not at all." It was silly not to try when they were already here.

When they arrived at Caroline's apartment building, Laura grabbed her cousin's phone and turned it on.

They caught Mr. Hillier, a spry senior with thick glasses, arriving home with a box of takeout. "Got a different car today, Caroline?" he asked Laura.

Laura explained who she was and asked him when he'd last seen Caroline.

"Not since yesterday morning," Mr. Hillier said. "I didn't see her car in the lot last night or this morning." His gaze shifted to Garrett. "She drives a red Firebird. Hard to miss."

"Did you notice anyone else go up to her apartment?" Garrett asked. "Or strangers enter the building?"

"No, it's been quiet around here all weekend."

Given the destruction in Caroline's apartment one floor above his, Garrett had to wonder how good the man's hearing was.

Laura pulled out the picture of Dwayne. "How about him?"

Mr. Hillier frowned. "This her ex?"

"Yes."

Mr. Hillier nodded. "She asked me a couple of weeks ago to alert her if I noticed him nosing around. Said he was taking the breakup pretty hard. Is she in trouble?"

"That's what we're trying to figure out." Laura pressed a business card into his hand. "Please call me if anyone else comes around asking after her."

The man slid the card into the breast pocket of his shirt, then patted it. "You can count on me."

As they headed back to his car parked on the street, Garrett floated the idea once more of asking the police to search the DMV for Dwayne's information. "We've clearly struck out. I'm not sure what else we can do."

Laura pursed her lips and lifted her chin, obviously still not ready to concede defeat.

They waited for a car to pass, then stepped out to cross the street.

"Caroline!" some guy shouted.

Laura whirled toward the voice.

A dark car barreled toward them, heading right for her.

9

"Watch out!" Garrett tackled Laura, pushing her out of the way as the car sped past, exactly where she'd been standing a moment before.

Laura scrambled to the curb on all fours, then spun around to check on Garrett. The man had saved her life. Again.

He clambered up behind her, wrapped an arm around her waist, and helped her to her feet. "Are you hurt?"

She swiped the grit from her hands and knees. "Just a little bruised. You?"

"The same." Garrett examined his leg. His pant leg was torn from his heel to his knee, and his calf was badly scraped. "I think the car's bumper clipped me."

Laura cringed. He could've been seriously hurt. That was not the action of a man with sinister intent. How had she ever doubted him?

He beeped the door unlock on his key fob. "I have a first aid kit in the car."

A man and a woman ran toward them.

"We saw the whole thing," the woman said. "It looked like the driver was aiming for you."

"I called the cops," the man said. "I didn't get the license plate, but it was a blue four-door Matrix."

"No, it was a black Hyundai," the woman countered.

The man shook his head. "A dark sedan of some kind then. I tried to snap a photo of it, but I couldn't get the camera on my phone activated fast enough."

"Appreciate the information." Garrett steered Laura past the pair and opened his car's passenger door. "Have a seat."

"You're the one who needs to sit," she said. "I'll get the first aid kit. Where is it?"

He hobbled to the trunk and retrieved it. "I'm going to have to stand. The scrape will be too hard to clean if I'm sitting."

Laura took the kit from him and rummaged through it until she found the antiseptic wipes. "Could you bend your knee and rest your foot on the seat?"

She gingerly rolled back Garrett's tattered pant leg, then dabbed the cool wipe against the raw skin. At his wince, she jerked her hand away. "Did I hurt you?"

"No, I'm fine."

Laura tried again, more cautiously this time. She swallowed hard. Maybe it was her imagination, but electricity seemed to hum between them. "Thank you for saving me."

"We'll get you some water from the corner store," the man volunteered. "Be right back."

With their audience temporarily gone, Laura succumbed to the compulsion to take Garrett into her confidence. After all, if she couldn't trust a man who would throw himself in front of a car to save her, whom could she trust?

"I need to tell you something," she said.

"What's that?" Garrett's voice sounded unusually husky, and she worried he was in more pain than he let on.

"Beth found a note from Caroline in that library book I returned."

"Why didn't you tell me?" The hurt in his voice almost undid her.

"Caroline warned me not to trust anyone. I didn't know what I should do."

Garrett groaned. "You thought she meant me?"

"Not counting your uncle's funeral, I've really only known you a couple of days. And you'd already come to my rescue twice. You've got to see how it could've felt orchestrated."

Before he could reply, a Pittsburgh police cruiser rounded the corner. The returning couple flagged it down. The cruiser parked behind Garrett's car, and a burly officer climbed out.

Laura was shocked to recognize piercing blue eyes behind the man's square-framed glasses. The same kind of glasses he'd worn when they'd been high school sweethearts more than a decade ago. He'd put on a bit of weight and gone prematurely gray, but the same old dimple winked in his cheek when he grinned.

"Laura, is that you?" Mel asked.

"Yes," she managed to squeak. "How are you doing?" Of the hundreds of cops Pittsburgh must employ, how was it that the one she least wanted to see responded to the call?

"Great." Mel closed the distance between them. "I'm married with three kids now. Every day is an adventure."

Like he always wanted.

Mel caught sight of the injury she was attending, and his face blanched. "You're the woman a driver tried to run down?"

"Yes. This is why I don't like big cities." She'd forced him to choose between her and becoming a big-city cop. She'd lost. "Garrett, this is an old friend from high school, Mel Tanner. Mel, this is Dr. Garrett Simons. He's taking over Doc's clinic."

"I heard about Doc's passing. That was too bad." Mel paused, then added more quietly, "Goes to show you that hit-and-run accidents can happen anywhere."

Thankfully the man who'd phoned the police jumped in with a description of the car, sparing her from having to respond to Mel's observation.

Mel took notes, then said, "I'll check street cameras in the vicinity. We might get lucky and catch a plate number. I assume you haven't made any enemies since I left Hopeton, so I'm guessing our eyewitness is exaggerating his claim the driver was aiming for you."

"You assume wrong," Garrett said. "The driver was aiming for her all right—or rather her cousin. He shouted 'Caroline' a moment before he gunned it."

"And I turned when I heard the shout," Laura filled in. "She's why I'm here."

Mel wrote feverishly in his notebook. "Do you and Caroline still look similar?"

"Very." Garrett took the bandage Laura was attempting to wind around his calf and sank onto the passenger seat, where he proceeded to wrap his leg himself. "And the guy didn't even try to stop."

"Yeah," the female witness agreed. "Now that you mention it, there was no sound of screeching brakes at all."

Garrett's gut physically ached at the thought of how close Laura had come to being run over. He'd been foolish to suggest they come here. "Do you trust Officer Tanner?" he asked Laura in an undertone. Something told him there was more to her history with the officer than mere friendship.

She nodded, pulled the mended photograph of Dwayne and Caroline from her purse, and handed it to Garrett. "I think we can."

Warmth shot through him at her use of the word *we*.

Garrett showed the cop Dwayne's picture. "Caroline has been missing since last night." He related the highlights of last night's incident at Laura's place. "We think Dwayne might be connected or at least know something. We assumed Caroline was kidnapped." He motioned to his leg. "But after this, it would seem she got away, and whoever was driving that car is still trying to find her."

Laura trembled, clearly unnerved.

Tanner studied the photo, then said to Laura, "You weren't expecting your cousin to visit you last night?"

"No, I'd asked a favor of her earlier in the day, but she said she couldn't do it. I was disappointed, probably sounded pretty annoyed over the phone. So when I first spotted her car outside my house, I figured she felt bad about refusing to help me and came by to make sure I wasn't mad at her."

"Dwayne could be tracking Caroline's phone," Garrett interjected. "She left it at Laura's place, but the battery was low. We charged it on the drive here this morning, and we switched it on again when we returned after eating."

"So you think he picked up the signal and assumed Caroline had returned?" Tanner concluded.

Garrett nodded. "I'm guessing he started watching the entrance, and when he saw Laura exit the building, he mistook her for Caroline."

"It's certainly possible," the officer said. "Phones are easy to track these days. Can I keep the photo?"

Garrett pulled out his phone and snapped a picture of the photo. "Now you can."

Tanner took down more information about the accident. By the time they were given permission to go, another officer was taking pictures and a news reporter with a camera had appeared.

They managed to leave the scene before the reporter clued in that they were the victims.

"Whew," Laura said as Garrett drove off. "We got away just in time."

"I hope so." Garrett was glad that Tanner had promised not to release their names, but that wouldn't stop people from recognizing them. "Maybe the cameras didn't capture images of us."

Laura stared at him. "You think Dwayne would try again?"

"If the driver was Dwayne, I'd be surprised if he didn't." Garrett motioned toward Caroline's cell phone sitting in the holder between their seats. "To be safe, you'll want to get all the information you need off her phone before we leave the area. We don't want him tracking it to Hopeton." *For all the good it would do.* He tightened his grip on the steering wheel. The man already knew where Laura lived from tracking Caroline there in the first place.

Garrett sensed perspiration beading on his forehead and his heart rate increasing, and he consciously slowed his breathing. He dropped his shoulders, willing the tension to drain away. He lifted each finger in turn from the steering wheel to relax his grip. He'd gotten pretty good at recognizing the onset of a panic attack in the months since the overseas incident had left him with PTSD. With some effort, he could divert himself from a meltdown. Unfortunately, the technique didn't work when he was sleeping.

His grip on the steering wheel reflexively tightened, and he walked himself through the relaxation exercise once more. He was grateful the attacks had never hit him in the middle of a stressful situation. The last thing Laura needed back there was his reaction to the situation scaring her more than the near miss.

Garrett slowly released another deep breath. If the loss of an innocent mother and son, villagers he scarcely knew, affected him this much, he hated to imagine how he'd ever cope if he lost someone he loved. He glanced over at Laura. One more reason not to let himself get entangled in a relationship.

A car horn jerked his attention back to the road, and he swerved out of the lane he'd drifted toward. He muffled a snort. Who was he kidding? He already cared more for Laura than any woman he knew—and he hardly knew her.

With a satisfied sigh, Laura put away the pen she'd been using to copy numbers from Caroline's phone, then powered it down. "I've copied her entire contact list and her outgoing call log."

"That's great."

Laura rested her head against the headrest. "We can rely on Mel. I'm sure he won't quit for the day until he's tracked Dwayne down."

Garrett nodded.

"Hopefully he'll take Dwayne into custody so Caroline will be safe. I was thinking maybe the reason she hasn't called is because she's afraid he'd monitor my cell, since he managed to track her to my house."

"Could be." Garrett hated to say anything to dampen the hope he heard creeping into Laura's voice. But the more he thought about the blank hard drive in Caroline's computer, the less sure he was that Caroline was running from Dwayne. Why would Dwayne erase the hard drive? "Who was the last person Caroline called?"

Laura consulted the list she'd made. "Not anyone in her contact list. Should I try calling the number?"

"Search for the number on your phone first."

A moment later, Laura said, "It's for a hardware store. Already closed for the day. I saw something in her journal about her looking for an antique claw-foot bathtub. Maybe this place tracked one down for her and she was planning to talk the building manager into letting her install it."

Garrett thought a call to a hardware store seemed innocuous enough. "Whom did she call before that?"

"Her friend Anita at the paper. She must've cleared all her earlier call history, like she did with incoming calls."

"What about texts?"

"All deleted. I do that from time to time when my phone gets sluggish."

Or there might be other reasons a senator's aide would do it. Garrett didn't want to say it out loud, but Laura's cousin had clearly gotten on the bad side of someone dangerous.

Laura flipped on the bedside lamp in Garrett's spare room. Garrett and his mother had insisted she stay with them another night. She hadn't wanted to impose, but Garrett overcame her reluctance by reminding her they still hadn't heard from Mel about Dwayne. At least she'd convinced Nancy to take the twin bed the movers had brought. Laura actually kind of liked sleeping on an air mattress. It reminded her of camping with Caroline in their backyards.

Laura grabbed Caroline's diary and snuggled under the blankets to read, hoping it would offer more clues to her disappearance. There were a few cryptic questions and notes jotted alongside random entries, such as, *Sold 10,000 shares the day before share price plummeted.* She assumed the notes had to do with Caroline's job—items she wanted to remember the next morning but couldn't be bothered to get out of bed to jot down on a notepad.

Laura's ringing cell phone startled her awake, and the journal tumbled to the floor. She squinted at the screen. It was after eleven. She must've fallen asleep reading. She connected the call.

"Sorry for calling so late," Mel said in a deeper baritone than she remembered from their high school days. "But I figured you'd want to know right away. I'm afraid I have bad news."

Laura shot up into a sitting position, and her blood roared so loudly in her ears that she could barely hear.

"I located Dwayne, but he doesn't drive a dark sedan. And he has an alibi for the time of the hit-and-run accident."

Laura nearly groaned aloud in frustration. Could the incident have been a random coincidence? Maybe the driver wasn't who had shouted her cousin's name. Maybe it was someone else calling to a totally different Caroline. "Does Dwayne have an alibi for last night?"

"I didn't ask," Mel said. "But I can pay him another visit in the morning."

"I appreciate it."

"Anything for you."

That sure hadn't been his tune when he'd had to choose between her and Pittsburgh. Disconnecting, she shook off the negative feeling. It was water under the bridge.

Garrett knocked at her slightly open door. "Was that your officer friend?"

"Yes." Laura pulled on her robe and joined him at the door. "Dwayne wasn't our driver. He has an alibi."

Garrett's heavy sigh mirrored her own frustration. "Hopefully your cousin will check in soon. I think the fact that someone mistook you for her is a good sign she wasn't caught by whoever followed her to your house last night."

"I hope so."

His gaze soft, Garrett gave Laura's shoulder a gentle squeeze, the warmth of his touch tempering the chill left by Mel's call. "Try to get some sleep."

After closing the door, Laura sat down and scrolled through her phone's call log to ensure she hadn't somehow missed a text or call from Caroline, since it would've come from a different number. But there was no record of a missed call. Trying not to think about what this meant, she returned to bed.

But she couldn't dismiss the reality that if Caroline was okay, she would've called by now.

Before Laura opened her eyes Sunday morning, she inhaled and snuggled a little deeper under the sheets, oddly comforted by the laundry soap scent—a scent that after this weekend would probably always remind her of the handsome ex-soldier who was determined to keep her safe. Knowing he was down the hall, ready to intercept any intruder, had helped her sleep better than she'd thought possible under the circumstances.

But now it was time to face the day. Laura showered and dressed in the outfit she'd brought from her house for church. Most of the women no longer wore dresses on Sunday mornings, but she liked the excuse to dress up after a week of diner wear.

By the time she entered the kitchen, Nancy was stirring a pot of oatmeal, and Garrett—incredibly handsome in gray slacks, a purple shirt, and a snazzy tie—was filling three mugs with coffee.

He whistled when he saw Laura. "You clean up nice."

Warmth crept into her cheeks. "Thank you. You don't do so badly yourself."

He dipped his head in gratitude.

"Would you like to join us for church?" Nancy asked. "We're going to Hopeton Community, where my sister attends."

"That's where I usually go," Laura said.

Garrett smiled as he handed her a cup of coffee.

Laura's stomach did a silly flip as her fingers brushed his. Taking a seat at the newly arrived kitchen table, she noticed two well-worn Bibles. If there'd been only one, she might've assumed it was his mother's, but this gave her the impression they both took their faith seriously. And that fact reassured her that confiding in Garrett had been the right thing to do.

Forty-five minutes later, they parked at the church. Laura usually preferred to walk, but they'd lingered too long over breakfast and Nancy had been worried it would be too hot to walk home by the time the service ended. Garrett opened the passenger's side door and offered his mother a hand while Laura climbed out of the back.

Her pulse jumped at the sight of Caroline's red Firebird rolling into the parking lot. "She's here," Laura squealed, pointing out the car to Garrett.

He squinted at the windshield. "The driver's a man."

Laura's breath stalled in her throat. "Why is Brian Schumacher driving Caroline's car?"

"Are you sure it's your cousin's car?" Nancy asked. "Perhaps it's just one that looks like it."

"With a ball on the tip of the antenna like Caroline's?" Laura fisted her hands and stalked toward Brian as he parked. "He's coveted my cousin's car since we were in high school."

Garrett jogged after her, catching up as she reached Brian.

"Where's Caroline?" Laura demanded the instant he stepped out of the car. "Why are you driving her car?"

He flashed Laura a victorious grin. "She stopped by my garage Friday night." To Garrett, he added, "I'm the town's mechanic, Brian Schumacher. We met at your uncle's funeral." He extended his hand, and Garrett shook it.

The traitor.

"She stopped by your garage," Laura prodded.

"She said she needed a new set of wheels," Brian continued. "She remembered how I'd always loved her car, so she offered me a trade for an SUV I had in the used lot beside my shop." He pressed his lips together. "Maybe you could forget I said that last part. I wasn't supposed to mention what car she got."

Laura stared at him, flabbergasted. This had to be good news, right? It explained why the police BOLO hadn't turned up Caroline's car. Also, it made it more likely that she was safe in hiding or at least on the run and not kidnapped. But . . .

"What are you thinking?" Garrett asked.

"Caroline loved her Firebird." She lowered her voice to a whisper. "She must have been seriously terrified to ditch it."

"You believe him?"

Laura sized up Brian. She'd known him since primary school. He'd tinkered with cars for as long as she could remember. Engine oil was perpetually embedded in the creases of his fingers. What would he want with Caroline, other than her car?

"Yeah, I guess I do." To Brian, she said, "Could I check inside the car? I might have lost my lipstick in there the last time Caroline gave me a ride." In her head, she could hear Caroline's voice taunting her about the lie.

He opened the passenger door for her. "Help yourself, but she said she'd had it detailed Friday morning."

"What kind of SUV did you sell Caroline?" Garrett asked.

"She didn't want me to say," Brian reminded him.

"Fair enough."

Laura stuck her hand in and under the seats, not sure what she was searching for but hopeful she'd know when she found it. Under the edge of the floor mat, she discovered a receipt for a coffee shop. The time stamped on it was mere hours before Laura had spotted the Firebird in front of her house. She opened the glove box, but it was empty save for an owner's manual. Figuring Brian would get too suspicious if she asked to see the trunk, Laura reluctantly got out.

Brian headed into church.

Garrett held Laura back. "Did you get anything?"

She showed him the receipt.

"The shop's phone number has the same exchange as the hardware store Caroline called. Remember? They could be in the same town."

"Which means she might have visited the hardware store before coming to Hopeton," Laura added.

Nancy ambled over to them from where she'd been waiting by her son's car. "Are you coming in?"

"You go ahead," Garrett suggested. "We might have a lead we need to follow. Do you think Jenny can give you a ride home?"

Nancy dismissed his concern with a wave of her hand. "Don't worry about me. You do what you need to do. We'll be praying you find her."

Garrett kissed her cheek. "Thanks."

After his mom left, Garrett asked Laura, "Are you okay with skipping church?"

Laura nodded, a tad guiltily. "I know I wouldn't be able to concentrate on the service for thinking about this possible lead."

"Time could be of the essence," Garrett said solemnly.

Getting back into Garrett's car, Laura reclaimed the front seat.

"You don't have Caroline's phone on you, do you?" he asked.

"It's in my purse, but it's still powered off."

"Good. Even though I was wrong about Dwayne using it to track Caroline's whereabouts yesterday, that doesn't mean no one else did."

Garrett typed the coffee shop's address into his maps app. "It's a twenty-minute drive. Do you want to change first?"

"No, I'm fine," Laura answered.

He navigated the town's side streets to the main road out of town. "I'm assuming you'd prefer not to tell the police about Caroline's vehicle switch."

"Yeah, she clearly didn't want anyone to know what she was driving."

"If neither she nor Brian went into the DMV yesterday to register the change in ownership, there will be no official record of it until at least Monday."

Laura gazed at the passing scenery, gripping the handle of the purse on her lap.

"Your cousin sounds like she knows how to take care of herself," Garrett reassured her. "Chances are she's holed up somewhere safe."

"What if our nosing around makes the situation worse instead of better?"

The wobble in Laura's voice made Garrett's soul ache. He eased his foot from the gas pedal. "It is a risk. Is it one you're willing to take?"

Laura drew in a deep breath and held it a long moment. "I need to know she's safe."

"Okay, let's go." He sped back up to the speed limit, and they soon reached the village of Bloomvale.

"There's the coffee shop." Laura pointed to a storefront halfway up the block that reminded him of a diner he would have expected to see in the fifties.

Garrett snagged the last available diagonal parking space in front of it.

The instant they entered the restaurant, the din of conversation grew silent.

"Sit where you like," the waitress called from the table she was clearing in the middle of the shop. "I'll be there in a second."

The customers resumed talking, this time in hushed whispers, with several slanting hostile glances in their direction.

"You get the impression we're not welcome?" Garrett murmured to Laura.

"I'm certainly not feeling the love." She smoothed her skirt. "Overdressed maybe?"

Garrett motioned to a booth that would allow them to have a private conversation with the waitress.

The middle-aged waitress bustled over with a coffeepot in hand. "I'm Alice. What can I get you folks?"

"Just coffee, thanks." Garrett flipped over the clean mug sitting on a saucer on the table in front of him, and Laura did the same.

While Alice filled Laura's cup, she said, "I didn't expect we'd see you back here anytime soon."

Laura's forehead wrinkled. "Pardon me?"

"You must be mistaking my friend for her cousin Caroline Brennan," Garrett interjected, exulted they'd hit the jackpot so quickly. "She was here on Friday."

"Oh." Alice squinted at Laura. "The resemblance is uncanny. Listen, I'm sorry for the scowls you're getting. I'm sure my customers made the same mistake. Most folks around here don't much care for the senator or anyone who works for her."

The elated look Laura flashed Garrett gave him a kick of energy stronger than any cup of joe.

"Do you happen to remember if my cousin came in with anyone?" Laura asked the waitress.

"Sure, she was having a heated conversation with Douglas Smythe. He owns the hardware store in town."

Garrett nodded. *That explains Caroline's call.*

"Is the store open on Sundays?" Laura asked.

"Opens in twenty minutes," Alice answered. "A word of advice—if you plan to talk to Douglas, take everything he says with a grain of salt.

He hasn't been quite right in the head since his brother died."

"How do you mean?" Garrett asked. As a doctor, he'd heard people use that expression for everything from a brain injury to the certainty that wearing magnetic jewelry was healing their arthritis symptoms.

"He's always on a crusade for one thing or another," Alice explained. "And that senator's aide resurrecting the memory for him didn't help things."

"How did his—?"

"Sorry, but I've got customers waiting for their bills." Alice hurried away before Garrett could quiz her on how Douglas's brother died.

"What do you think?" Laura asked.

He smiled, ridiculously pleased by her interest in his opinion. "I think we need to talk to Douglas Smythe."

"Me too." She checked her phone. "Mel still hasn't gotten back to me on Dwayne's alibi for Friday night, but it seems more likely that what's going on has to do with Caroline's work for the senator."

"I agree." He motioned to her coffee. "Drink up, and we'll head over there."

Alice must've informed the other patrons of Laura's true identity as she topped up their coffees, because the hostile stares subsided.

Garrett left a generous tip, and they gave the other customers polite nods as they walked out.

"That went well," he said with a chuckle.

Laura shuddered. "I haven't been so glad to leave a place since I had my wisdom teeth pulled."

Garrett laughed. He adored her sense of humor and loved that she could keep it given how worried she was about her cousin.

As they walked the half block to the hardware store, Garrett couldn't help but notice how the sunshine made Laura's hair shimmer.

The building must have been constructed in the early 1900s and hadn't been updated in more than half a century. The front window had posters for an era of products before Garrett's father's time.

"This seems more like an antique store than a hardware store," Laura commented.

"It's antique all right." A tinny bell jingled as Garrett opened the door for her.

The floors were wooden and noticeably sloped. The walls were cluttered with products from floor to ceiling, and judging by the sliding pegboards, those were two and three panels thick.

A squat gray-haired man hurried out from a back room. "Good afternoon—" The instant the man caught sight of Laura, he blanched. "Caroline?"

11

Laura had the sickening feeling Douglas Smythe thought he was seeing a ghost. If he believed Caroline would never set foot in his hardware store again, what did he think happened to her?

Once again Garrett stepped in and explained her relationship to Caroline.

Douglas visibly relaxed.

"What did my cousin discuss with you when she came to town?" Laura asked.

"She wanted to revisit an interview we did six years ago when she was still a reporter," Douglas replied. "Fat lot of good the article did us. But she was probably already conniving to become one of the senator's flunkies back then."

"What was the article about?" Garrett asked.

"I thought it was going to be about my brother blowing the whistle on PrimeCorp," Douglas said. "But it turned out to be about a bunch of industrial polluters, and the real story got buried in the rhetoric."

Laura's breath caught. She'd had a niggling feeling the scribbled question about PrimeCorp they'd found in Caroline's trash can had to be significant. "What exactly did your brother see PrimeCorp doing that was illegal?"

"What weren't they doing? If you ask me, the senator was in on the cover-up. But there was no mention of that in Caroline's article."

"How do you figure?" Garrett asked.

The man jabbed his index finger into the counter. "When

PrimeCorp wouldn't make the needed pollution-control changes my brother brought to the management's attention, he went straight to the senator with his concerns. Before anything could be done about the situation, he plummeted to his death in a so-called industrial accident."

"I'm so sorry," Laura said.

"I don't believe for a minute it was an accident," Douglas said. "My brother was the most safety-conscious person in the entire place. I think they rigged the chain to snap so the girder would fall on him."

Murder? Laura glanced at Garrett. Was this what the diner waitress had meant when she warned them to take everything Douglas said with a grain of salt?

"There must've been an investigation," Garrett said. "What did it conclude?"

"Unforeseen metal fatigue." Douglas grimaced, then reached under the counter and slapped a container of mixed screws on the counter. He began to sort them as he continued. "To add insult to injury, PrimeCorp got nothing but a token fine."

"I can certainly understand why that would anger you," Laura said. "Did PrimeCorp ever clean up its act? With regard to the pollution, I mean?"

"Why would they if the senator's going to give them a pass? Pollution control costs money. They won't do anything that'll hurt their bottom line unless they have to."

"How do you know this?" Laura asked. "Do you have other family members working there?"

"I watch them, and I see what's going on." Douglas gestured toward the newspaper rack next to the checkout counter. "When the story of my brother's death hit the papers, followed by the decision to fine PrimeCorp, their stocks plummeted. In the end, they made a fortune off the whole thing."

"What do you mean?" Garrett asked.

"They bought back their stocks at rock-bottom prices," Douglas said. "Once the incident blew over and the stock value rose again, they sold them at a tidy profit."

Laura pictured the notation Caroline had made in her journal about something like that. Had she been writing about PrimeCorp stocks?

"I'm still a little confused," Laura admitted. "If Caroline wrote the original article, what did she hope to learn by interviewing you again?"

"She knew I keep my eye on PrimeCorp," Douglas replied. "I write letters to the editor and senator about them all the time. Not that it does any good. The senator likely sent her here to shut me up. Caroline acted sympathetic, as if she wanted to see PrimeCorp exposed, but I know that's all it was—an act."

"I can't believe my cousin would lie about her intentions," Laura said.

"Did she seem nervous, like someone was following her when you spoke?" Garrett asked.

Douglas's hand stopped in midair, the screw he'd been about to put into a container pinched between his fingers. "Now that you mention it, she was kind of jumpy. Kept looking out the window and at the door when people came. We were in the coffee shop, so people went in and out the whole time."

"I got the impression a lot of people in town didn't like her," Garrett remarked. "Do you know anyone who'd try to hurt her?"

Douglas shrugged.

"Would *you*?" Laura asked.

Douglas scowled. "Of course not. I may not like her boss's politics, but unlike PrimeCorp, I don't shoot the messenger." He scratched his beard. "But it's as if everyone who asks too many questions winds up dead. Like that doctor in Hopeton."

"What do you know about Dr. London's death?" Garrett demanded.

Douglas took a step backward, his hands lifting in surrender or innocence or fear. "Just what Caroline told me. It was a hit-and-run accident, and the driver was never apprehended."

"Why would Caroline talk to you about Doc?" Laura asked.

Grateful at least one of them was thinking straight, Garrett took a moment to rein in his rising temper.

"When she asked me about PrimeCorp," Douglas said, "I told her I wasn't the only one digging into their dirty little secrets, so she asked me what I meant. I told her about Dr. London calling me. He said he'd read my letters to the editor and asked if I knew what my brother had on PrimeCorp before he died. He said he was compiling proof that might finally put a stop to PrimeCorp's corner cutting."

"What kind of proof?" Garrett asked.

"Since he's a doctor, I assumed something to do with medical conditions employees were developing as a result of the work environment, but I don't know. It was a busy day in the store when he called, so I answered his questions and didn't ask any of my own. I figured we'd talk again."

"Did Caroline seem surprised by Doc's interest in PrimeCorp?" Laura asked.

Douglas frowned, his gaze straying, as if he were picturing the exchange in his mind. "No, I don't think so. But I was surprised when she told me he was dead. She'd asked me what he'd told me, and I told her to talk to him."

"Which might explain her sudden decision to visit me," Laura said to Garrett.

He gritted his teeth in an effort to keep his emotions in check. "So, let me get this straight. You believe PrimeCorp killed Dr. London to silence him."

"I wouldn't put it past them," Douglas said. "They orchestrated my brother's accident because he tried to blow the whistle on them."

"Do you think they would go after Caroline?" Garrett raked his fingers through his hair. What was he asking? Of course the man did. He clearly thought PrimeCorp was evil incarnate. If Uncle Richard had managed to pry useful information out of him, why hadn't PrimeCorp taken out Douglas Smythe—the biggest thorn in their side, if he could be believed?

"Nah. Not while she's working for the senator. And the senator is championing their bid for an upcoming military contract." Douglas snorted disdainfully. "For some reason, she thinks keeping a few hundred jobs in the state and lining the pockets of one of our biggest corporations is more important than the health of our environment and people."

Garrett was beginning to see why PrimeCorp might have opted to leave Douglas alone. If they let him spout long enough, he started to sound a little too crazy for most people to believe, whereas if they silenced him, they might wind up turning him into a martyr for his cause.

A family came into the store and asked about camping equipment.

"Excuse me," Douglas said to Laura and Garrett. "I need to help these customers."

Garrett waited a few minutes, hoping the family would soon tire of browsing, but it quickly became clear they weren't leaving until they'd outfitted their entire trip—tents, sleeping bags, camp stove, canoe, and more.

"We might as well go," Garrett said to Laura. He thanked Douglas for his time as they passed him on the way to the door.

"Are you as freaked out as I am?" Laura asked the minute they were outside.

"That's a good way to describe it." He touched the small of her back to guide her across the street while the road was clear, without a single idling car in sight. From here on out, he intended to keep his head on a swivel, constantly assessing the scene as he'd learned to do in war zones.

"Do you think PrimeCorp is after Caroline because she won't pander to the senator's expectations?" Laura asked.

"Not sure they are the senator's expectations. But PrimeCorp likely has a vested interest in Caroline *not* digging up dirt on them to report to the senator."

"Either way, it could be why Caroline's gone into hiding." Laura grabbed his arm. "What if PrimeCorp paid off the police too? Maybe that's why Lieutenant Reynolds was so insistent I ID the driver they pulled from the truck they recovered."

Garrett clenched his fists, wishing he could punch something. Reaching his car, he inspected it for tampering, as inconspicuously as possible so as not to worry Laura more. Finding no evidence of sabotage, he opened the door for her and waited until she was safely inside before rounding the car and sliding behind the wheel.

"I'm not sure how much of what Douglas Smythe says is grounded in fact," Garrett said, "and how much is his imagination."

"But your uncle called him," Laura pointed out. "Douglas wouldn't lie about that. He brought it up, not us."

Garrett drove slowly out of town, remaining on high alert for anything suspicious. If PrimeCorp did have something to do with Richard's death, they might be searching for the evidence he'd compiled. Maybe they thought he had it on him when he died and might have given it to Laura when he realized he was dying. It would explain why the man had accosted her at the cemetery, demanding a file. It might also explain the recent break-in at the clinic.

Only why wait six weeks? Was it because Laura hadn't followed their script and confirmed the corpse was his uncle's killer?

For most of the drive home from Bloomvale, Garrett mulled over their conversation with Douglas Smythe. The more he thought about it, the more he didn't like what it could mean. "I have a bad feeling Douglas was right about my uncle dying for asking too many questions."

"I don't understand why Doc was curious about PrimeCorp," Laura said. "I don't know of anyone in town who works there, so I doubt any of his patients suffered an industrial accident on the job. If they did, I'm sure the weekly paper would've reported on it."

"Richard made frequent trips to the library to research everything from rainfall records to the dates of aerial spraying of pesticides," Garrett said. "Beth told me that he wanted an explanation for an uptick in patients from south of town with strange symptoms."

"You mean people like Herbert MacKenzie? He was in the diner complaining about the new doctor pushing pills to treat symptoms, instead of trying to figure out what was really wrong."

"That's not good. I'll have to review Dr. Henri's cases." He slapped his palm to the steering wheel. "Except I can't, because my computer backup doesn't have the last six weeks. I'll have to ask her if she kept any written notes."

"The pharmacist could tell you what prescriptions she's written in that time," she suggested.

"That's a start. Maybe she can work backward from those records to help reconstruct the missing data."

"Another customer referenced a young girl with strange symptoms, including a rash, and the doctor prescribed antidepressants for her," Laura said. "She didn't mention the girl's name."

"When we get back to the house, I'll go through Mr. MacKenzie's medical records and see what Uncle Richard wrote in his file," Garrett said. "Maybe it will shed some light on the potential causes he'd hoped his library hunt would confirm. If Douglas can be believed, my uncle likely suspected the cause had something to do with PrimeCorp."

Laura frowned.

"We'll figure this out. And find your cousin."

Laura's acknowledging smile and slight nod triggered inexplicable emotions in Garrett. He returned his attention to driving, but he couldn't resist one more glance in her direction. She was beautiful. She caught him watching her and ducked her head, her impossibly long lashes sweeping her cheeks. Okay, maybe his emotions weren't so inexplicable.

The house was quiet when they returned, since his mother was spending the afternoon with his aunt.

"Want some lunch before we start?" Garrett pulled a loaf of bread from the cupboard and then opened the fridge. "I'm sure I have the fixings for a sandwich."

Laura went to the sink and washed her hands. "Let me take care of making sandwiches and coffee while you set up your laptop."

"Good plan. We can work at the kitchen table."

He returned with his laptop and USB backup. She looked at home in his kitchen. He'd miss having her around when she went back to her house. They made a good team.

Laura sliced the turkey for sandwiches. "I was thinking about the note we found in Caroline's trash can. Do you know anyone in the army who might be able to tell us if PrimeCorp had a contract with them?"

"I can call my former army commander. He might know or at least know someone who does." Without sitting down at the table, Garrett stole a bite of the sandwich she set next to his laptop. "I'll grab my phone."

Scrolling through his contact list, he hoped the man was still stateside.

Commander Adams answered on the second ring. "Didn't expect to hear from you. Tired of civilian life already?"

"No sir."

"You've been having more trouble with . . . ?" Adams let the rest of his question trail off.

But Garrett knew he was referring to the PTSD he'd suffered since their last overseas mission. "I'm handling it," he said tersely, peeking at Laura to see if she'd overheard the question. Thankfully she seemed focused on doctoring their coffees. "The reason I'm calling, sir—"

"You can stop the 'sir' stuff," Adams said, interrupting him. "You're not in the army anymore."

"Habit. I'm wondering if you can tell me what a company by the name of PrimeCorp supplies the army."

"Munitions."

"Is that a recent contract?"

"We've contracted with them for years," Adams said. "But suppliers change."

"Do you know if their manufacturing process produces anything that would be a health concern?"

"I don't imagine factories are the healthiest environments to work in."

"I was thinking more of the pollution the factory might produce," Garrett said. "Like maybe noxious gases or chemical waste?"

"That would be for other government bodies to monitor."

They talked for a few moments longer about mutual acquaintances.

When he disconnected, Laura asked, "Do you think PrimeCorp's factory is close enough to Hopeton that pollution from its stacks would affect our health?"

"I don't know," Garrett replied, "but it might be something my uncle was investigating. Beth said he asked for rainfall records. We know acid rain is a widespread by-product of poor pollution controls. Maybe PrimeCorp is producing something that gets past the scrubbers American factories are required to have in their stacks."

They ate in silence as Garrett found Herbert MacKenzie's medical file. "My uncle has noted a lot of peripheral details about the man that you typically don't see in a medical record."

"Like what?"

"The fact his house is on well water. They live in a sixty-year-old brick bungalow, no asbestos that they know of. His hobbies in addition to all of his former occupations. Whether they've ever detected mold in the house, which Herbert said they hadn't, other than a bit of mildew from time to time on bathroom tiles."

"I can see why Herbert appreciated how thorough Doc was," Laura said. "He was working hard to discover a cause of Herbert's ailments."

"Yeah, if it had only been an eighty-five-year-old man with strange symptoms, Richard might've chalked them up to old age. But younger people, like the girl you mentioned, had them too, so he knew there had to be more to it."

"Perhaps we should talk to your aunt," Laura suggested. "Maybe she's come across your uncle's notes. Does he have a laptop at home?"

"I asked Jenny that already," Garrett answered, "but she said he never brought his work home. He put in long enough hours at the office and hospital, and he didn't think it was fair to let his work spill over into their home life."

"But he did work at the library, so he might've carried a flash drive in his pocket with information he collected. Did you check his phone? I often take pictures with mine of garden designs I like for future reference. Maybe he took pictures of some of the reference materials he used."

"I didn't think of asking Jenny about either of those." Garrett finished his sandwich and coffee. "Let's do that now."

Matt Stephenson was the last person Laura expected to see at Jenny London's house. As Garrett parked, Laura wondered whether he knew of Matt's connection to Doc's death.

"That must be the young man from church my aunt said volunteered to help her with yard work," Garrett said. "You know him?"

"Yes, Matt's a really nice guy."

"I'll say. I can tell you when I was his age, the last thing I wanted to do on the weekend was yard work." Garrett opened Laura's car door for her, then went over and shook Matt's hand, introducing himself. "I appreciate your helping my aunt this way."

Matt glanced at Laura before dropping his gaze back to the hedge clippers he'd been using. "It's the least I can do."

Laura didn't miss the guilt in his tone. As Garrett headed for the porch, Laura patted Matt's arm encouragingly and whispered, "This is a very nice thing you're doing, but do it because you care about Mrs. London, not out of a sense of guilt, okay?"

Matt nodded, but his hollow eyes said guilt was still eating at him.

At least he'd found a constructive way to work through it. She silently prayed he succeeded. Too many people resorted to far more self-destructive ways of coping with such feelings.

Jenny opened the door ahead of Garrett's knock. "Your mom's already gone back to your place. A friend of mine joined us for lunch and gave her a ride. You must've just missed her."

"We actually stopped by to ask if you happened to come across a USB drive when you went through Uncle Richard's things. Perhaps in one of his pockets." Garrett explained what they thought Doc might have been researching regarding patient symptoms, but he left out their suspicion that it could be connected to PrimeCorp and possibly his death.

"I'm afraid I haven't been able to bring myself to sort through his clothes yet," Jenny admitted.

"Do you happen to have his phone?" Laura asked.

"No, that was never recovered from the accident scene," Jenny said. "The police weren't convinced he'd had it on him, since they weren't able to find it, although they admitted it could've gone flying when he was struck and perhaps went down a storm drain."

"Or maybe someone picked it up and kept it," Laura said.

A pained expression crossed Jenny's face, as if she didn't want to believe anyone in Hopeton could be so callous. "You're welcome to go through Richard's jacket pockets and such. I could tell he was frustrated with not being able to figure out what was causing a sudden cascade of seemingly unrelated ailments in several of his patients. But we didn't discuss it much."

When they entered the house, Jenny showed them to the master bedroom. "His clothes are on the right side of the closet and in the highboy. Can I get you some lemonade?"

Because Laura suspected Jenny wanted an excuse to escape, she said she'd love some lemonade.

Garrett agreed. After his aunt left the room, he asked, "How about you get the closet and I'll take the dresser drawers?"

"Works for me." Laura started by reaching into each jacket pocket. Fortunately, unlike hers, they were devoid of candy wrappers. Not so fortunately, they were also devoid of anything else too, aside from the odd coin. She tried the breast pockets of his shirts next. They were all laundered and pressed, so not surprisingly she found their pockets empty. Same with the pants.

Dropping onto all fours, Laura scoured the closet floor for anything that might've fallen out and noticed cleavers clinging to a pair of pants that must have dropped from the hanger or merely been tossed into the closet. But cleavers weren't a plant he'd have readily come into contact with in town. Her curiosity piqued, Laura inspected the bottoms of the men's shoes lining the floor of the closet. The hiking shoes had mud caked into the treads and the dried blossom of a wildflower.

Laura surged to her feet. "I may know how to figure out where Doc was before he died."

"How?" Garrett asked.

Laura showed him the hiking shoes. "This blossom and the cleavers I found on his pants indicate he's been hiking through a woodland."

Garrett groaned. "Hopeton is surrounded by woodlands."

"Yes, but your uncle shared my love of plants, and one day he was asking me about the identity of a plant he'd come across. I told him about the plant ID apps available."

"But that doesn't help us. We don't have his phone, remember?"

"Let me finish." She headed back to the kitchen, where she'd left her purse.

"Ready for your lemonade?" Jenny asked. "I made up a plate of cookies too."

"That's lovely." Laura helped herself to a seat at the kitchen table and opened the plant ID app on her phone.

"Did you find anything helpful?" Jenny asked.

"Maybe." Laura logged in to her account. "Doc wanted to try a plant ID app without going through the rigmarole of setting up an account, so he downloaded the same app I have, and I added him as a second user to my account."

Garrett joined her at the table and sat where he could view her phone screen. "Does that mean you have a record of the plants he examined?"

"It sure does," Laura said. "The way the app works is you take a picture with your phone, and the program searches its database to provide a best guess of what the plant is."

Garrett sighed. "But how does that tell us where he saw the plant?"

"Ah, that's the best part. If you have your phone's location service on, it also records the GPS coordinates at the time the plant picture was taken." Laura scrolled through the list of dates Doc had accessed the app. "Bingo." Grinning, she paused to help herself to a cookie. "He accessed the app the day he died."

"Let's see what he photographed," Garrett urged, sounding impatient.

Jenny pulled up the chair on the other side of Laura to look too.

Laura scrolled down the photo thumbnails to the most recent. "You're not going to believe this."

"What in the world?" Garrett gaped at the image—not of plants but of leaking industrial barrels in a wooded area. What had Uncle Richard stumbled onto? "He didn't tell you about seeing this?" he asked his aunt.

Jenny appeared as flabbergasted as he felt. "Not a word."

"The picture was snapped less than an hour before the accident," Laura said. "He probably never had the chance."

"Where is this?" Garrett demanded.

Laura clicked on the app's GPS coordinates for the image, and it brought up a map pinpointing the exact location. "South of town."

Garrett nodded. It was the same area in which his uncle's patients with the mysterious ailments lived. "I want to check it out."

Jenny worried her bottom lip. "Are you sure that's safe? Perhaps you should show this to the police."

"The police could be in on the cover-up," Laura said.

His aunt blanched. "Cover-up? What are you talking about?"

Garrett frowned at Laura, then took a few seconds to calm himself before taking his aunt's hands. "If the chemicals leaking from those barrels got into the soil or stream, it could've caused the symptoms Uncle Richard saw in his patients. I think the burglary at the office might have to do with them too. Earlier today we talked to a guy who said Richard told him he was compiling evidence to put a stop to a company's corner cutting."

"That sounds like something your uncle would do," Jenny said.

"Do you think the police already knew about the leaking barrels and didn't want the information to get out?" She gulped. "Maybe they lied about not finding Richard's phone too."

"That's a real possibility," Laura said.

Garrett couldn't help noticing she'd avoided meeting his gaze before she answered, making him regret his overreaction to her suggestion of a cover-up. But he hadn't wanted to needlessly worry his aunt, or worse, speculate that Uncle Richard was murdered, only to discover later it wasn't true.

Garrett pushed to his feet. "We should get going."

"You haven't touched your lemonade," Jenny protested.

Garrett dutifully gulped it down and grabbed a cookie to go. "Thanks. Don't worry. I'll let you know what we learn." He kissed his aunt's cheek and motioned for Laura to precede him out the door.

When Garrett saw Matt still hard at work in the front yard, Garrett detoured over to him. "Could you do me a favor and give me a call if you see anyone suspicious watching the place?" He handed him a business card. "My phone number is on the bottom."

Matt stared at the card.

"Okay?" Garrett asked.

Matt tucked the card into his hip pocket. "Yeah, sure. I can do that."

By the time Garrett reached the car, Laura was already buckled up.

"We'll need to change into hiking clothes and shoes before we go," she said.

"I don't think it's a good idea for you to come."

Laura smiled. "Then it's a good thing I'm an adult and can make my own decisions."

"Stumbling onto those barrels in the woods could've been what got Richard run down."

"Yeah, that's what I'm thinking."

"If we're right, being spotted there could paint a target on our backs. I can't let you—" He clamped his jaw shut at the irritation on her face when he glanced her way.

"Can't let me what? Put myself in danger? Between the attack at the cemetery and then my house, I'd say I'm already in this up to my eyeballs. Wouldn't you? Not to mention they might already have my cousin."

Garrett couldn't argue with that. "Fine."

"Besides, if it wasn't for me, you wouldn't know where to search," Laura continued. "And I know these woods far better than you do."

"I agreed already."

She sat back in her seat. "Right then. Let's go home."

Home. He liked the sound of that more than he should have. He let the silence drag on as he drove to his house.

As Garrett parked in his driveway, he decided to make a last-ditch attempt to change her mind. "In the army, we learned to retreat if we were in over our head."

Laura rolled her eyes.

He slapped the steering wheel. "Okay, yes, I'm being a control freak. But I'm a control freak who cares about you."

She seemed to soften at his heartfelt words, but rather than acquiesce, she merely whispered, "I appreciate your concern."

Garrett expelled a sigh and opened his car door. As a military man, admitting defeat didn't come easy, but he figured this might be a situation where he was better off forfeiting the battle than losing the war.

He walked Laura to her door, wanting to ensure no new intruders were waiting for her. Once satisfied the house was empty, he left her to get changed and went home to do the same. His mom was napping, so he wrote her a note, saying he and Laura were going for a hike and they'd be back by supper.

Twenty minutes later, they blazed a trail through the woods south of town, slapping at mosquitoes and fighting off prickly raspberry bushes.

After ten minutes of hiking with no sign of the barrels his uncle had photographed, Garrett said, "I don't see any cleavers around here."

"They die back after they go to seed."

"How close are we to the GPS coordinates on the photo?"

Laura checked her phone. "Just up ahead." They entered a small clearing. "This is the place."

"There are no barrels," Garrett said, stating the obvious.

She stooped down and studied the flora underfoot. "No, but this is new plant growth. It's indicative of an area that was recently disturbed—such as in the past six weeks."

"You're sure?"

"Positive."

"So, whoever dumped those barrels here in the first place must've decided they needed to relocate the evidence Richard found." Garrett pointed to an overgrown trail, wide enough for them to walk side by side. "This way."

As they walked, he remained on high alert for any sound or sight to suggest they were being watched. When they heard nothing other than birdsong and the babbling river, he started to relax. "What sparked your love of plants?"

"My granddad." Laura beamed at the memory. "He loved to garden, and I loved to be with him. He patiently explained everything from how to plant seeds to the best way to keep weeds under control. But his favorite garden was the flower bed he planted for my grandmother every year."

"Oh?"

"She loved to decorate the house with cut flowers and take bouquets to the sick or shut-ins, so my grandad spent a lot of time making sure there was always a rainbow of long-stemmed flowers in bloom all summer long."

He smiled. "The garden must've been beautiful." Almost as beautiful as the light in Laura's eyes as she described it.

"Breathtaking. And it smelled divine."

"Why didn't you go into horticulture? You're obviously passionate about it."

"When did you first know you wanted to be a doctor?" she asked.

Curious about why she'd abruptly changed the subject, Garrett hesitated a moment before answering. "When I was five. My best friend lost his arm in a farm accident, and he had to spend weeks in the hospital. I visited him a lot and kept saying how cool the doctors were. His parents invited me to go with him when he got fitted for his prosthetic arm, and I saw therapists working with all kinds of kids suffering from various missing limbs. It was a real eye-opener. I decided then and there that I wanted to help people like that when I grew up."

"I guess you didn't see many kids while in the army."

He stroked his jaw to mask the tic in the muscle—a reflexive reaction to the memory of the last child he'd treated. Treated and lost, along with the boy's mother. "There were a few." He cleared his throat.

Laura stopped in her tracks, her gaze shifting from the scenery to him. "While overseas?"

Garrett nodded, silently cursing the incessant tic in his jaw.

"Civilians?"

Her concern surprised him. "Yes. In remote areas, we were often the only medical option available to them."

"Are we talking things like delivering babies and setting a broken bone? Or were these children hit by bombs and mortar fire?"

Somehow she'd managed to capture his worst nightmare in one simple question. Except that it hadn't been a nightmare. It had been all too real. "Yes." To his horror, his voice cracked. He forced himself to slow his breathing and shut out the images of that day.

Laura touched his arm. "I'm sorry," she whispered.

Garrett swallowed. "Me too." He held back a branch for her as he tried to dissipate the pressure building in his chest by repeatedly flexing and opening his other hand. If he'd needed any more proof that he wasn't ready to contemplate a relationship, he had it. He couldn't even be open with her about the gist of what he'd seen without risking a panic attack.

"I can't imagine how difficult that must have been," she said.

Unfortunately, it still is.

Laura chewed on her bottom lip. The anguish in Garrett's voice was palpable. She hated to imagine what he must've been through, even as part of her wondered if what he needed most was to be able to talk about it.

"You asked me why I didn't pursue a career in horticulture," she said, changing the subject once more. After the torment she'd clearly resurrected with her questions, the least she could do was answer his question. "My dream was to have a career that involved my love of plants and gardening. After Dad died, Mom needed my help with the diner, and it never seemed right to abandon her."

She supposed she'd been a lot like Matt in that way, feeling as if she'd owed that much to Mom, since Dad never would've been in Pittsburgh the night he was attacked if she hadn't begged to go to the hockey game.

"You've been working at the diner since high school?" Garrett asked.

"Yeah, I took it over from my mom a few years ago when her arthritis became too debilitating for her to keep working."

"Now that your mom's retired, why not sell the diner?" Garrett asked. "You could use the proceeds to pursue your dream, start a garden design business or something."

Her heart skipped a beat at the suggestion, then ached. She shook her head. "I can't. I'm too old to start over."

"I'm starting over, and I suspect I'm older than you."

"I don't know. Selling the place would feel like I was letting Dad die all over again. Dad's Diner is the only thing we have left of him."

"Is that how your mom feels too?"

"I've never talked to her about it."

"You should."

Laura squirmed and mentally cast about for another topic of conversation.

"I know a lot of fathers hope their children will take over the family business one day," Garrett went on. "They can get pretty upset if their kids want to forge their own paths. But my dad always told me I had to live my life, not his, and that meant I had to follow my own dreams."

"What did your dad do?"

"He owned an electrical repair shop," he said. "That was back in the days when appliances and electronics weren't built by robots and could still be repaired without spending more on parts than it cost to buy the item new."

She chuckled. "So, taking over your dad's business wasn't particularly viable?"

"Not really. Thankfully he was able to sell the store property for a nice chunk of coin to feather his and Mom's retirement nest."

"Do you—?"

Garrett suddenly stopped and pressed his finger to his lips.

Laura froze, listening intently. Sensing nothing amiss, she whispered, "What did you hear?"

"I caught a whiff of cigarette smoke," he said.

Laura inhaled. "Yes, I smell it too." She turned, sniffing again. "It's coming from the direction of the road. Someone might've flicked their cigarette out the window as they drove by."

"Hear that?" Garrett asked.

Voices. Her pulse quickened. It could merely be a couple of hikers, but her gut wasn't buying the explanation.

Garrett picked up two heavy limbs and handed one to her. "Stay alert," he ordered. "And stay close."

This time Laura didn't question his authoritative attitude. He had far more experience evading the enemy than she had. And it was kind of reassuring. They'd seen no sign of the barrels Doc had photographed. But from the width of the trail they'd been following, a truck could have easily been driven to the clearing to haul the barrels away. Proving as much was another matter.

Garrett veered off the trail toward the sound of the voices.

She grabbed the back of his shirt. "What are you doing? Aren't we trying to avoid them?"

"It's face them or wait them out, because my car is that way."

Laura slapped at a mosquito and scratched at the numerous bites she already had. At this rate they'd be eaten alive by bugs if they waited. "Okay, let's go."

Garrett set off again, this time at a faster clip. She stuck close behind him.

When they neared the road, Garrett stopped and peered through the trees. "It's a police cruiser."

Laura swept back the leaves to see for herself. The cruiser was parked behind Garrett's car, and the officer was standing on the shoulder of the road talking to a woman. Laura could only see their backs, but the woman seemed familiar. She stood a few inches under six feet, with dyed white hair, and she was slightly overweight.

Laura mentally flipped through the customers that regularly came through her diner but couldn't place the woman. Still, she was certain she recognized her.

The woman turned slightly.

At the sight of her large black-framed glasses, Laura gasped. "It's Senator Funk."

"Caroline's boss?"

"Yes." Laura struggled to draw in a full breath. "What's she doing here?"

Garrett held out his arm as they cleared the woods and stepped onto the road. "Stay behind me."

"I highly doubt Lieutenant Reynolds plans to shoot us on a public highway," Laura said.

Garrett hoped she was right. "What's going on?" he called to the lieutenant and senator while there were still a good fifty yards between them. "Are there parking regulations along this road I don't know about?"

Senator Funk frowned. She wore a pristine white pantsuit, no doubt designer quality. And Garrett couldn't help but wonder if it was meant to subconsciously send the message she was as pure as the driven snow. He snorted. More like she wasn't about to let any dirt stick to her. The woman was even more intimidating in person than on TV. She had a reputation for being tenacious, and rumor had it she'd be vying for a candidacy in the next presidential race.

"Who are *you*?" the senator demanded.

"Dr. Garrett Simons, ma'am."

The senator turned to his companion. "And you're Laura? Caroline's cousin?"

"That's right."

The tension in the woman's posture eased at Laura's confirmation. "Were you looking for Caroline in the woods? Have you found a clue to her whereabouts?"

"No," Laura said a little too quickly, the pitch of her voice giving away her nervousness at being caught out here.

Garrett hoped the senator would interpret it as concern for Caroline.

Laura must've realized her gaffe, because she ducked her head and added more softly, "Not a one."

"You found her car. Why didn't you report it?" Lieutenant Reynolds asked. "We still had a BOLO on it, and staking out a church parking lot to see who'd climb into it was a waste of resources."

"Sorry. That was an oversight." *Sort of.* Garrett could see why not calling would irritate the man. But the fact Reynolds had gone to the trouble to locate the vehicle didn't necessarily make Garrett feel good about him. He might simply be pursuing Caroline on her pursuers' behalf.

"My receptionist passed along the lieutenant's message about Caroline being missing," Senator Funk said to Laura. "Since I was attending a nearby retreat this weekend, I stopped in at the police department, and Lieutenant Reynolds took me to your house. Your neighbor spotted the cruiser in your driveway and came to tell us you'd gone hiking in the woods to search for Caroline."

"That would be my mother," Garrett interjected. "I'm afraid she was napping when we left and must've misunderstood the note I left telling her that we were going for a hike. We needed to get out into nature for a while. Laura has been stressed all weekend, worrying about her cousin."

Laura nodded.

"I'm so sorry." The senator touched Laura's arm. "Caroline's disappearance is deeply concerning to me as well." She straightened and displayed the trademark expression she always wore when cameras were rolling. "Now that I'm aware of the situation, I will use all the resources at my disposal to locate Caroline."

"I appreciate that." Laura chewed her bottom lip. "But . . ."

Garrett tensed, hoping Laura wasn't going to confide in the senator. Surely Laura believed her cousin's warning applied to a politician.

"I did learn my cousin recently broke up with her boyfriend," Laura admitted quietly. "I'm hoping that means she simply wanted a little getaway."

Garrett mentally applauded the diversion tactic.

"You were assaulted in your home," Reynolds reminded Laura. "By someone you thought was after your cousin."

"I was rattled," Laura said. "Now that I've had time to consider it, I think you were right that I must have surprised a would-be burglar."

Reynolds scowled. He clearly wasn't prepared—or perhaps able—to accept Laura's backpedaling now that the senator was involved. The dark smudges beneath his eyes and his crumpled shirt betrayed a tiredness Garrett hadn't perceived in him Friday night.

"But you saw your cousin's car in front of your house," Reynolds went on. "She left her phone in your home, then abruptly sold her car. Why would she run off like that?"

The senator nodded. "Caroline loved that car. To part with it, she must have been a lot more desperate than needing to get away from an ex-boyfriend."

"He has a reputation for being a bit of a stalker," Garrett offered.

"All the more reason to call the police," Lieutenant Reynolds said.

Since it seemed clear Laura wasn't going to convince Reynolds to back off, Garrett decided on a different tack that might glean some useful information from the senator. "Could Caroline's disappearance have something to do with her work?"

The senator grimaced. "As my aide, Caroline is privy to sensitive information. If certain information got into the wrong hands, it could lead to serious consequences."

The trill of a cell phone caused everyone to check their phones.

"It's mine," Laura said, returning her phone to her pocket. "It can go to voice mail."

"I should be heading back to Pittsburgh," Senator Funk admitted, sounding genuinely reluctant. She dug through her designer handbag. "I don't plan to wait until tomorrow morning to learn whether your theory about Caroline is right. My people will start tracking her down right away."

"Thank you," Laura said.

The senator closed her handbag, then pressed a business card into Laura's hand. "This number is my direct line. Please call me immediately if you hear from Caroline or if I can assist you in any way."

The muscle in Reynolds's jaw tightened. "You should leave the search to the police. We don't want you endangering yourself."

"I agree." Garrett reached for Laura's hand and gave it a squeeze, hoping she got the message to let them go. "But please keep us updated. As I said, Laura's been very worried."

Reynolds nodded, then opened his passenger side door and motioned for Senator Funk to climb in.

"We'll find her," the senator said encouragingly to Laura before Reynolds shut the door.

Laura's clasp on Garrett's hand tightened, and he reflexively stroked his thumb across it. Her skin was surprisingly soft, given her passion for gardening.

As Reynolds drove away, Laura's grip relaxed, and her hand slipped from his grasp. "That was Mel who called before." She pulled her phone from her pocket and tapped the screen. "I need to call him back. He said he'd talk to Dwayne again first thing this morning, and it's almost suppertime."

"I'm glad you didn't take the call while they were standing here."

"I didn't want to have to explain whatever update Mel has."

"You told the senator your suspicions about the ex," he reminded her. "I was surprised you divulged that much."

"Senator Funk was being so kind, I felt as if we had to say something more. And since we were going around Pittsburgh asking about Dwayne, I figured she might hear about it anyway. This way, she'll think his being after Caroline is still our main assumption and forget about seeing us in these woods."

"Speaking of which," Garrett murmured, "we should vamoose before the wrong people catch us snooping." *If they haven't already.*

Laura climbed into the car, but as if she'd read his thoughts, she said, "I don't like Reynolds. There was an undercurrent of tension or something running between him and the senator. Did you notice?"

"I noticed he was singing a different tune than he was Friday night." Garrett turned his car back toward town. "I'm not sure how, but I'd like to look into whether PrimeCorp was one of the senator's campaign contributors."

"You think she knows about the illegal dumping?"

"I don't know. She didn't press us on where we'd walked, nor was she particularly antsy about our being in the woods. But if PrimeCorp is one of her backers, she'd have a vested interest in keeping a lid on its alleged illicit activities."

Laura shook her head. "I can't see Caroline working for anyone that unscrupulous."

"Maybe she didn't know until now. I'm not saying it's true. But a run at the presidency requires deep-pocketed financial backers—backers who'd expect to be kept happy."

Laura returned Mel's call since he'd left no message beyond asking her to phone him. When his voice mail picked up on the first ring, she said, "Hi, it's Laura. Sorry I couldn't take your call a few moments ago. I was talking to the senator. Please call me back as soon as you can."

While she waited for him, she did an Internet search on donor contributions to Senator Edwina Funk. "Oh, this is interesting. There's a new super PAC in support of Funk."

"Remind me what a super PAC is," Garrett said.

"Independent expenditure-only committees. They're allowed to raise unlimited sums of money from corporations, unions, associations, and individuals, and they spend it to advocate for or against political candidates, through ads and commercials and such. But they can't donate the money directly to a political candidate or coordinate their spending with one."

"So what's the deal with this super PAC?"

"Its number one contributor is Nathan Carruthers, founder of PrimeCorp. He's given millions of dollars."

"That definitely smacks of collusion."

"Yes, but it doesn't mean the senator knows what PrimeCorp is doing. Carruthers could be positioning himself to call in a favor when needed. Maybe for his son, Brad." Even with the magnitude of the numbers staring her in the face, Laura hated to think ill of Senator Funk. She'd seemed genuinely concerned about Caroline.

Garrett bypassed their street and continued to Main Street.

"Where are you going?"

"In the note I left my mom, I told her we'd pick up fish and chips for supper. You like fish?"

"Love it." Except she couldn't stay with Garrett indefinitely. It had been two nights, and he was already taking for granted that they'd share dinner. Not that she minded. She was going to miss having someone to eat with once they found Caroline and this was all over.

Laura examined his fingers, curled around the steering wheel. When he'd reached for her hand back there on the road, she'd felt as if a bevy of butterflies had taken flight inside her—a reaction she hadn't had to a guy's touch since Mel first held her hand in high school. Oh, she'd dated people casually over the years, but those relationships had run their courses without much emotional expenditure.

It had to be her concern for Caroline throwing her emotions out of whack. Because she didn't want to be attracted to Garrett. He was nice enough. He always remembered to hold doors for her and urged her to follow her dreams. And he was certainly handsome. She hadn't thought she liked crew cuts much, but on Garrett, with the whispers of gray at the temples, it was classic. Of course, with his lean, muscular build and chiseled features, any haircut would probably work for him.

Laura stifled a sigh. She was starting to think like Beth. Her friend would be going nuts right now if she knew Garrett had held her hand.

Not that Laura was reading anything romantic into his motive for doing so. If she was smart, she wouldn't tell Beth about it at all. Her happily engaged friend was already bad enough with her incessant matchmaking attempts.

"Are you all right?"

Realizing Garrett had already parked at the fish and chips shop, Laura shook the thoughts from her head. "Pardon?"

Garrett chuckled. "You were miles away. I asked if you wanted one piece of fish or two."

"One is enough for me."

"Be right back."

The shop was across the street and three doors down from the diner. Laura tilted her head and scrutinized her storefront, still the same as it had been when she was a kid, except that the red-and-white awning had faded to pink and gray. It was probably time she invested in a new one. Her gaze strayed farther down the street to where the pickup had struck Doc. Her breath caught. *It's him.*

She froze, even though he wasn't looking her way. He was studying the diner. She quietly opened the car door and slipped out for a better view. It was definitely the guy who'd run Doc down—blond hair swept to one side and three days' worth of beard growth. What should she do?

Laura started toward him.

He pressed his phone to his ear and headed the other direction.

When he turned the corner out of sight, Laura broke into a run. She couldn't let him get away. The blood roared in her ears. Reaching the corner, she skidded to a stop and peered around it. He was gone.

Footfalls pounded the ground behind her.

She spun around, arms raised.

Garrett caught her by the forearms. "What are you doing?"

Laura exhaled. "Oh, it's you."

"Who were you expecting?"

"I saw him. I saw the driver who ran down Doc."

Garrett tightened his grip on her arms. "And you thought you'd chase him down? What were you thinking?"

She tugged her arms from his grip. "I was thinking he needed to be caught."

"You should've come and gotten me," he said, clenching his jaw.

"There was no time." Laura motioned to the empty street. "As it was, he got away."

"You're sure it was him?"

"Positive."

"Not a smart move on his part," Garrett said. "He must know the police have a witness who can ID him."

She headed toward the only store on the side street open on a Sunday.

"Where are you going?" he asked, matching her strides.

"To see if I can find him."

Garrett made an exasperated noise. "Promise me you won't confront him. If you spot him again, we fall back and call the police. Deal?"

Laura tilted her head and surveyed Garrett. "You could take him. You have at least two inches on him."

"Thanks for the vote of confidence, but I don't want him to see you."

Then it was a good thing Garrett didn't know the guy had been casing her diner before she started after him.

Laura stepped into the variety store to search for the driver, but any hope of remaining incognito was ruined by her phone's loud ring. Every person in the small store glanced her way. The man she'd hoped to find wasn't among them.

Laura exited the store to take the call from Mel. "What did you learn?"

"Sorry it took me all day," Mel said. "I never managed to get ahold of Dwayne. His neighbor says he left early this morning to vacation at his family's cottage on the lake near Hopeton." He gave her the address in case she wanted to ask the local police to pay him a visit.

Laura thanked him, then updated Garrett, who'd positioned himself between her and the street, making constant visual sweeps of the area. Now that the adrenaline had worn off from her initial sighting of the hit-and-run driver, she could see how worried Garrett was that she'd become the guy's next target. She doubted they'd locate him now unless they went door-to-door. Part of her wanted to do just that, but prudence won out.

"We'd better get the fish and chips home to your mom," she said.

During the short drive home, Garrett said, "You weren't thinking of going to see Dwayne, were you?"

Laura shook her head. "Since Caroline probably went into hiding because of what she figured out about PrimeCorp, I think it'd be a waste of time."

"Good, because I had another idea. After supper we could visit Brian Schumacher and ask him if the SUV he traded for Caroline's Firebird had a GPS locator on it."

"That's a fabulous idea. I wish we'd thought of it this morning."

Garrett parked in front of his house and collected the boxes of food from the back seat. "Let's hope Lieutenant Reynolds didn't."

Her chest tightened. If he had, would he have bothered to bring the senator out for her? Or could that have been a diversion? Laura took a deep breath, then slowly exhaled. She wished Caroline had told her why she shouldn't trust anyone. Now she felt paranoid.

He stood at her open car door. "You okay?"

"Yes, sorry. Collecting my thoughts."

Nancy greeted them at the door. "Did the senator catch up with you? She was very concerned about your cousin."

"Yes, we spoke to her." Garrett led the way to the kitchen. He set the boxes on the table and put on coffee.

"I hope you didn't mind that I told them where you went," Nancy said as she retrieved cups and plates from the cupboard.

"If anyone else comes around asking after Laura or me," Garrett said, "it might be better if you don't say anything about where we are."

Laura fumbled her cup with a bone-jarring rattle. Was he worried about the hit-and-run driver tracking her here? She'd never forgive herself if accepting these kind people's hospitality endangered them.

"You're going out again?" Nancy asked.

Laura couldn't decide if Nancy sounded pleased or disappointed. Laura felt bad for taking Garrett away from her when she'd come all this way to spend time with him.

"Yes," Garrett said. "There's something we need to check out."

Over dinner they talked in generalities about their day, and Nancy told them about the sermon and her visit with Jenny. Laura savored the dinner conversation. She'd miss it when she went back to living under her own roof.

After the last French fry was eaten, Laura gathered the dirty plates.

"Leave the dishes," Nancy said. "I'll take care of them."

Garrett rose and kissed his mom's cheek. "We might be a while, but we should be home before dark. You'll be okay?"

She waved away his concern and smiled at Laura. "Of course. I'm in the middle of a good mystery book."

Laura wished the mystery of the disappearing cousin were fictional. "Do you think it's safe to leave your mom home alone?" she whispered as she and Garrett put on their shoes at the door.

"We'll be back before dark," Garrett reiterated, as if that made all the difference.

Laura decided not to remind him that dusk had scarcely set in when the intruder had attacked her Friday night.

They found Brian at his house next to his business and learned the SUV he gave Caroline did have a GPS tracking system. Best of all, he still had the code needed to access the information in real time.

"You can get the app on your phone, and I can show you how it works. Or we can check it on my phone." Brian opened the app on his phone and input the required code. "Looks as if she's by the lake."

There was only one lake near Hopeton—the same lake where Caroline's ex had supposedly gone that morning.

Brian watched his phone screen for a good twenty seconds, then added, "The SUV appears to be parked."

"I'll download the app to my phone so we can monitor its position in case she decides to move," Garrett said.

"Did you show this to anyone else?" Laura asked the mechanic.

"You mean like the cop? Nah. I couldn't deny I'd seen Caroline, since I was climbing into her Firebird right there in the church parking lot when he found me. But once I proved she'd signed the car over to me, my memory got fuzzy." He grinned.

Laura chuckled, grateful he'd told her when Caroline had clearly convinced him to stay mum.

Garrett showed Laura the newly loaded and working app on his phone. "We're good to go."

They thanked Brian for his help and returned to Garrett's car.

"What if someone's tracking *your* car?" Laura said. "We could lead them right to Caroline."

Garrett scanned the vicinity. "I suppose it's possible. I haven't noticed any suspicious vehicles following us, but if I do, we could lead them on a merry chase."

She noticed the twinkle in his eye, and it eased her worry. "Okay, let's do this."

The lake was a thirty-minute drive from town, and Laura estimated it would take another ten to fifteen minutes on the winding dirt road circling the lake until they reached Caroline's location. During the drive, Laura divided her time between monitoring the GPS app and watching the side mirror for a tail. As they neared the lake, the map zoomed in, revealing the names of the various lanes off the main road around the water.

When Laura read the name of the lane where Caroline's vehicle blipped on the screen, her breath stalled in her throat. "Dwayne has her."

"What?" Garrett slowed the car.

"The GPS shows the vehicle on Aspen Lane," Laura explained. "That's where Dwayne's cottage is."

He pulled to the side of the road. "But your cop friend said he couldn't have been the driver who ran us down outside Caroline's apartment, and Dwayne doesn't have anything to do with PrimeCorp."

"Not that we know of. Or maybe we were wrong about the two incidents being connected." She pointed to the blinking dot on the map. "Because Caroline's SUV is parked at his cottage."

"She could've decided to hide out there," Garrett suggested. "The last place Caroline would expect someone to check for her is at her ex-boyfriend's."

"That's true. If her friend from the paper hadn't made him out to be a stalker, I wouldn't have known she'd even had a boyfriend."

"So, we keep going?"

"I think we have to," Laura answered. "I need to know if she's okay."

Garrett pulled onto the road. He'd better be right about her cousin asking for her ex's help, because the last thing he wanted to do was walk Laura into a hostage situation. But if Dwayne was as into Caroline as her friend made out, she could've figured he'd be happy to help, and she could deal with his inevitable hopes that they'd get back together later.

A vehicle swerved onto the dirt road ahead of them, kicking up a cloud of dust. Garrett's thoughts flashed to the sandstorm in Iraq. The mother and son. So much blood. He felt as if he couldn't drag enough air into his lungs. The child's cries deafened him.

Road dust blasted the windshield, reducing visibility to near zero. Garrett gripped the steering wheel and stomped on the brakes.

"What's wrong?" Laura asked.

"I can't see!" he yelled above the roar in his ears.

"But—"

"I know what I'm doing." Gritting his teeth, Garrett forced his breathing to slow—in through the nostrils and out through pursed lips. As he began to calm down, he loosened his grip on the steering wheel.

The dust had cleared.

He slanted a sheepish glance in Laura's direction.

She'd backed against the car door, her expression wary.

Garrett bit back a curse. He should explain, but that was the last thing he wanted to do. "Sorry," he muttered and stepped on the gas.

"Slow down," Laura said. "Aspen Lane is ahead on the left."

The lane was badly rutted. He slowed to a crawl.

Garrett stopped a hundred yards short of the driveway. "I want you to stay here until I make sure it's safe."

"Forget it. Caroline is my cousin. We'll do this together."

"What if you're right about Dwayne and he's holding your cousin captive?" he asked. "We're no good to her if we're both caught. This way if you don't get the all clear from me, you can call the cops."

"We don't know if the cops are on our side," she argued. "What if Caroline came here to hide out? She doesn't know you. She might think PrimeCorp sent you. She's not going to show herself."

Garrett shook his head. "I still don't think it's a good idea."

"If Dwayne's as volatile as Caroline's friend said and he thinks you're here to hurt Caroline, he might strike first and ask questions later," Laura continued. "The smartest thing to do is let me go in. If Caroline is safe, she'll know me. If Dwayne is holding her hostage, he won't see me as a significant threat." She flashed him a smile verging on sardonic. "In which case, you can come to our rescue."

"I'm not letting you go in there alone," he insisted.

Laura opened her car door. "Suit yourself. But I'm going to see my cousin."

Garrett reached for her arm, but he caught empty air. He jumped out of the vehicle and rounded the car. "Be reasonable."

"I'm being perfectly reasonable." Her response came out in a subdued hiss as she quietly shut her door.

He supposed he should be grateful she was at least cognizant of not alerting them to their arrival too soon.

"You're the one who's not making sense," Laura added. "From the way you're suddenly acting, how do I know you haven't been stringing me along this entire time, using me to get to Caroline?"

The accusation stung. "Now you're being ridiculous."

"Am I?" She propped her hand on her hip and stared at him.

"Okay, we'll do it your way," Garrett relented. "But let's at least scope the perimeter together before you go in."

They made their way soundlessly down the lane to the driveway.

"There it is." Laura motioned to a blue SUV parked in front of a small clapboard cabin.

"There are two other recent sets of tire tracks." Garrett pointed to the smaller ones. "Looks as if an economy-size car was parked next to the SUV." He gestured to larger tracks at the tail end of the driveway. The vehicle must have spun out, digging the tracks deeper into the dirt. "These ones are from a bigger vehicle."

"Could've been from someone turning around in the driveway," Laura speculated.

"Maybe." He studied the visible windows. "I can't see movement inside."

"They could be sitting by the lake or out on a boat," Laura whispered.

Garrett found a sturdy branch to carry, in case they needed to fend off an attack, then led the way around the cabin, leaving a wide berth of cover between them and the building. "There's a boat tied to the dock." And there was no sign of anyone outside. "They might have gone somewhere in the second vehicle." He squinted at the large picture window on the back of the cabin, overlooking the lake.

"I'll try knocking." Laura stepped from the cover of the trees.

Fractionally more confident they'd find Caroline without incident, he palmed his phone and hurried after her.

She took the veranda stairs two at a time and knocked on the door. The door opened a crack. "Caroline, are you there? It's Laura. I've been worried about you."

A groan sounded from inside.

"Caroline?" Laura's voice rose in agitation.

Garrett managed to catch her arm before she went inside. "That didn't sound like a woman's groan." He urged Laura to stand to the side of the doorframe, then nudged the door open a little more. "Caroline? Dwayne? This is Dr. Simons, Laura's neighbor. Is someone injured? I can help."

Laura grabbed Garrett's shoulder, snapping his attention to her.

Her face ashen, she pointed at the gap in the door at an angle opposite to his line of view.

Garrett shoved the door the rest of the way open. Dwayne lay on the floor, blood staining the front of his shirt, his breath raspy. "He's been shot." Garrett pressed his phone into Laura's hand. "Call 911."

Laura rushed out the door.

Resisting the impulse to run to the man's aid, Garrett eased around the corner of the doorframe, his branch weapon held at the ready. "Caroline, are you in here?"

No response. No sound at all save for Dwayne's strangled breaths and groans.

Spotting a pistol near the man's side, Garrett picked it up and opened the chamber. It was fully loaded. After slapping it shut, he dropped the branch and finished searching the cabin for the shooter and Caroline.

Laura dashed inside. "Help is on the way. Did you find Caroline?"

"She's not here." Garrett shoved the gun into the back of his waistband, then snatched a beach towel hanging over a chair. He sank to his knees at Dwayne's side and pressed the towel to the hole in the man's chest. "Hang on."

Dwayne gasped, and his eyes fluttered open.

"Where's my cousin?" Laura demanded. "Where's Caroline?"

"They took her," Dwayne said, his voice hollow with despair.

16

"Keep pressure on his chest." Garrett pressed Laura's hand against the towel he'd been holding to Dwayne's bullet wound. Feeling for the man's pulse with one hand, Garrett pried back an eyelid with the other. His pulse was thready.

"Who shot you?" Laura asked Dwayne. "Who took Caroline?"

"She . . . she called me. From a convenience store." Dwayne's chest barely rose with each inhale.

"He's going into shock." Garrett raced into the bedroom and grabbed a blanket and a pillow from the bed. He propped Dwayne's legs on the pillow, then covered him with the blanket.

"Stay with us," Laura urged the injured man.

"I'll take over." Garrett relieved Laura of having to apply pressure to the wound.

"What did Caroline say?" Laura asked.

"She . . . said she needed a place to hide out for a couple of days." Dwayne struggled for his next breath. "Asked to stay here. I . . . wasn't supposed to . . . come. Not safe."

"Who shot you?" Laura repeated, leaning over them. "Who took Caroline?"

"Drove a black truck. She . . . said—" Dwayne groaned and went limp.

"What did she say?" Laura wailed. "Who has my cousin?"

Abandoning the towel, Garrett began CPR.

"If we'd gotten here sooner, we could've stopped them." Laura's tone verged on hysterical.

Garrett blew a long breath into Dwayne's lungs, then said sternly, "Or we could've all been shot. Now pull yourself together. I need you to apply pressure to the towel, so I can do chest compressions without him bleeding out."

Falling silent, Laura dropped to her knees and did as Garrett instructed.

Sirens blared in the distance.

Mentally counting the compressions, Garrett fought to stay in the present. But everything—from Laura's low keening to the acrid smell of blood—sucked him back to that day. He'd promised the boy he wouldn't let his mother die. "She's not going to die!" Garrett slammed his fist into the man's chest to kick-start his heart and resumed compressions. "I won't let her. I promise I won't let her."

Laura was taken aback. Was Garrett talking about Caroline? He seemed to be caught in some sort of nightmare, struggling to revive Dwayne but thinking of Caroline. Or was he reliving another trauma?

A crack from the region of Dwayne's rib cage made her jump. "Garrett?" she said softly, but he didn't respond.

She'd heard him cry out in his sleep the first night she'd slept under his roof. She'd seen enough war movies depicting veterans haunted by their dreams that she hadn't thought much about it. But the tortured crease of his brow threatened to undo her.

Garrett continued the compressions at a frenetic pace. "Don't give up on me!" he yelled at Dwayne.

"He's gone," Laura whispered. "We were too late."

"Keep the pressure on that wound," he ordered.

"You've got to understand that every second longer we spend here, the farther away they're getting with Caroline," she said. "The car that stirred up the dust storm ahead of us was probably them racing away."

Garrett glanced at her. "The police will blockade the road."

At least he'd responded to what she was saying. "It could be too late by then." Laura gripped the blood-drenched towel. They'd wasted too much time arguing already. She should've known a car careening at that speed on these dirt roads couldn't have been up to any good.

The sound of sirens grew closer. Would the cops chase down Caroline's kidnappers? She doubted it.

Laura sprang to her feet. "We need to go. Now."

"What?" Garrett stared at her as if she'd grown a second head. "We can't leave him."

"He's gone, but there's still time to save Caroline." Using the one clean corner of the beach towel, she wiped the blood from her hands as best she could.

"I can save him. Keep pressure on that wound."

The sirens grew louder.

Laura frowned at Dwayne's still body, guilt squeezing her chest. "We have to let him go."

"The ambulance is almost here." He steadily continued compressions.

She reluctantly resumed pressing the towel to Dwayne's wound.

The cabin door burst open, and two policemen charged inside.

Laura jumped up and spun around.

"Stop! Hands in the air."

Laura raised her hands. "You have to set up a blockade. The kidnappers are getting away with my cousin. They shot Dwayne and took off with her. We saw them leaving, but we didn't realize they had Caroline."

"Down on the floor," the cop ordered. His name tag read *Jones*. "Hands on the back of your head."

"Where's the ambulance?" Garrett asked, ignoring the order.

"Down on the floor," Officer Jones repeated.

"Haven't you been listening?" Laura slapped her hands to the back of her head. "We didn't do this. We thought we'd find my cousin here. She's been missing since Friday night. You've got to believe us. Dwayne was still alive when we arrived. He told us what happened. We tried to save him, but we were too late."

"We're not too late," Garrett said, his voice defiant.

The second cop's name tag read *Benson*. He ordered Garrett to the floor, then shouted, "Gun!"

Jones turned his weapon on Garrett, and Benson confiscated the gun and wrestled Garrett to the floor.

"You can't do this," Garrett protested. "I'm trying to help him."

"He's a doctor!" Laura screamed.

"Get down," Officer Jones told her. "Now."

Laura obeyed this time.

"Clear!" Jones yelled toward the door.

Two paramedics raced inside and went to work on Dwayne.

Within minutes, one of the paramedics sat back on his heels and shook his head. "He's dead. From a single gunshot wound by the looks of it."

"We didn't shoot him. The gun was Dwayne's," Laura desperately explained to Officer Jones, now frisking her for hidden weapons. "Garrett picked it up when he came inside, because we didn't know if Dwayne would try to shoot us or if anyone else was still here." Why wasn't Garrett saying anything?

She heard the click of handcuffs snapping onto his wrists. A moment later, Officer Jones twisted her arms behind her back and slapped cold steel on her wrists too. "You're under arrest on suspicion of murder."

"I'm the one who called 911," Laura argued. "Would I have done that if I shot the guy and was trying to get away?"

Officer Jones clasped her arm and tugged. "On your feet."

Laura stumbled as the cop wrenched her around to walk out the door. She noticed a tattoo on the inside of Benson's arm—the same tattoo she'd seen on her intruder's arm Friday night.

Knowing better than to talk, Garrett had been numbly compliant as Officer Benson frisked and cuffed him.

Laura abruptly stopped talking, and the silence snapped Garrett to attention.

The cop escorting him toward the cabin door pushed him forward, but Garrett resisted, craning his neck until he could see Laura behind him and satisfy himself the officer handling her wasn't threatening her in any way.

The sight of her deathly pallor triggered a fresh shot of adrenaline. "Check the gun," he said. "It hasn't been fired. Everything Laura said is true. You need to blockade the road now if you want to catch the real shooter."

Laura glared at him, and with the tiniest of movements, shook her head.

Garrett was confused. Had she decided not to trust the police?

Benson shoved him out the cabin door, and Garrett squinted against the light. Only one police cruiser was parked in the driveway, and an ambulance sat on the shoulder of the narrow lane. Garrett silently thanked the Lord for small mercies. At least he and Laura would be taken to the police station together.

Benson opened the back door of the cruiser, then set his palm on the top of Garrett's head and pushed him inside. Laura joined him from the opposite side of the car.

The doors slammed, and the locks clicked. But Officers Benson and Jones returned to the cabin rather than climbing into the front.

"I'm sorry," Garrett said. "I'm afraid they don't intend to blockade the road. Not when they're convinced they've already got their murderer."

Laura twisted in her seat, her gaze sweeping every inch of the car's interior. "Do you think they bug the inside of the vehicle?" she whispered.

"I don't think so, but I know officers in certain jurisdictions wear body cameras and some have them on the dash. I'm not sure how much sound they'd pick up. Why?"

She leaned close. "Something really rank is going on here. Did you see the tattoo on Benson's arm?"

Garrett's thoughts flailed. He'd had his face planted on the floor most of the time. He pictured the cop reaching past him to open the car door. His sleeve had slid up his arm, revealing some sort of tattoo. "Yes. What about it?"

"I recognized it. He's the intruder who attacked me at my house Friday night—the one after Caroline."

"He's a cop."

"You've never heard of dirty cops?" Laura asked.

"Sure, but almost everyone sports a tattoo these days. How can you be sure he's the same guy? You never mentioned a tattoo Friday night."

"I didn't remember it until I saw the cop's arm. He had the same looping script on the inside of his wrist as Friday night's intruder. It has to be the same guy."

"You think Benson is working in cahoots with whoever nabbed Caroline?"

"He has to be," she said. "When they arrived, you were doing CPR on Dwayne, and I was holding a towel to his side. Anyone with two eyes would've known we were trying to help him."

"If I'd had more time, I might've been able to—"

"His death isn't your fault," Laura insisted. "You did everything you could."

Garrett sighed, attempting to see the scene from the officers' viewpoint. Did they really think he shot Dwayne and then tried to save him? Or had they been stalling for time to ensure Caroline's captors got away before a blockade could stop them?

"I'm telling you that cop's dirty," Laura hissed, as if she'd had the same thought.

"Here he comes," Garrett whispered.

Benson climbed into the driver's seat and started the engine.

When he started to back out of the driveway, Laura asked, "You're leaving without Officer Jones?"

Garrett's stomach clenched at the ripple of fear underscoring her question.

"He's waiting on the forensics team," Benson said in a careless tone, but it sounded forced. "We didn't want to leave you cooking in a hot car longer than necessary."

"We appreciate that," Garrett said. He wished his hands weren't cuffed behind his back, so he could clasp Laura's hand and reassure her. Because from the panicked glances she was tossing at every window, he suspected she was convinced the last place Benson intended to take them was the police station.

Garrett pressed his leg against hers. "It's going to be okay."

She nodded, but her audible gulp told him she didn't believe it.

Twenty minutes later, Officer Benson parked outside the police station. The one small mercy was it wasn't in Hopeton. And with any luck, there wouldn't be any reporters around, or Garrett's career as a small-town doctor would be over before it started. It would be next to impossible to win the trust of his new patients if they heard he'd been hauled into jail on suspicion of murder.

But that wasn't what concerned him most. *I don't care about me, Lord. Just please help Laura get out of this and find her cousin safe.*

The last time Garrett had bargained with God, he'd survived, but the mother and child he'd been trying to save hadn't. Survivor's guilt, some called it. It had almost been enough to make him lose his faith. But after he'd climbed out of the abyss of self-pity he'd been wallowing in, he realized he'd seen too many miraculous answers to prayers on other occasions to shut out God. Unfortunately, the realization didn't make reality hurt any less.

A female cop met the cruiser and escorted Laura inside the station, where she was taken to a different room than Garrett. He was searched again, swabbed for gunshot residue, and fingerprinted.

"I want to call my attorney," Garrett said repeatedly throughout the process.

Eventually they handed him a phone. Of course, besides the real estate lawyer he'd hired to close the deal on his new house, he didn't know a lawyer. He considered calling his mother, but he quickly nixed that idea. There was one other phone number he had memorized—the army base.

He dialed the number and asked to speak to Commander Adams.

Within minutes, he had the man's assurance he'd have an attorney there pronto.

The officer shut Garrett in a claustrophobic room to await his lawyer. Garrett hoped Laura had contacted someone too.

Good to the commander's word, William Harris—a grizzled, white-haired man in a crisp charcoal-gray suit—arrived within the hour. The attorney conferred with Garrett to ascertain the facts of the case, then invited the officer to ask his questions.

Benson walked in and unlocked Garrett's handcuffs. "You're free to go. You can collect your belongings at the front desk."

"You're dropping the charges?" William clarified.

"The gun found in his possession hadn't been fired, and there was no gunshot residue on his hands or clothes, so we have no evidence to link him to the shooting," Benson explained. "It appears that it happened as he claimed. He arrived after the fact and tried to save the victim's life." No apology. No emotion in the officer's voice at all. He merely recited the facts as if reading from a script.

William clapped Garrett on the back. "That was the easiest case I've had in a while. Let me know if you need me again."

"What about Laura?" Garrett asked. "Where is she?"

Benson shrugged. "I imagine she's gone home." He escorted Garrett and his attorney to the front desk, then gave Garrett a receipt to reclaim his belongings.

When the officer left, Garrett stopped William from doing the same. "Please don't go until we know where Laura is." He lowered his voice. "She believes that officer is the man who broke into her house Friday night looking for her cousin."

William widened his eyes.

"I'm afraid he might have made her disappear rather than release her."

"When's the last time you saw her?" William asked.

"Over an hour and a half ago. A female officer took her to another room." Garrett handed the receipt to the desk clerk.

The clerk gave Garrett a sealed plastic bag containing his belongings and another receipt. "Take this to the impound on Sixth Street to retrieve your car."

Garrett's pulse jumped. If Laura had already been released, she wouldn't have had any way home—the perfect excuse for one of Benson's minions to volunteer to take her.

"What's your friend's name?" William asked Garrett.

"Laura Brennan."

William tapped on the front desk and handed the clerk his business card. "I'm here to confer with my client. Laura Brennan was brought in an hour and a half ago."

The clerk consulted his computer. "Sorry, sir. She was released about twenty minutes ago."

"Did you see her?" William asked. "Did she report here to collect her belongings?"

"I haven't been here that long. One moment." He tapped a few keys on his computer keyboard, then thumbed through the tote from which he'd retrieved Garrett's belongings. "Her things were collected."

William thanked the clerk, then escorted Garrett toward the door. "Do you have Laura's number?"

Garrett snatched his phone from the bag and tried to power it on. "It's dead."

"I have a charger in my car. You can call from there while I drive you to the impound to get your car."

Garrett studied the foyer as they left the police station, hoping against hope to find Laura waiting for him. But there was no sign of her.

Laura would have hung around to wait for him. Then again, given how desperate she'd been to locate her cousin, she might not have.

Outside, he scanned the streets. Again, there was no sign of her.

The instant Garrett climbed inside the lawyer's car, he plugged in his phone and impatiently waited for it to charge enough to come on. He dialed her number, and her phone began to ring. Once, twice, three times. "Pick up."

But he got her voice mail after the fourth ring, inviting him to leave a message.

"Laura, where are you? I've been released, and I'm on my way to the impound to pick up my car." Garrett disconnected as William pulled out of the parking lot. "Where are you going? Sixth Street is the other direction."

"You passed my street," Laura told her cabdriver from the back seat.

The driver stopped his meter and glanced at the rearview mirror. "Sorry. I'll go around the block."

Laura tensed. Something about his tone felt wrong. Her phone rang, and she jumped. Nerves made her hands unsteady, and it felt as if it took her ages to fish the phone from her purse and read the screen. Relief swamped her at the sight of Garrett's name, and she rushed to connect the call.

But he'd already disconnected. She tapped his name to return the call, then realized the cabdriver wasn't slowing to take the next street. She clutched the back of his seat. "Hey, you need to turn here. You can take this street back around."

Laura tried to call Garrett, but his line came up busy. He was probably leaving her a voice mail. She sent him a text, then returned her phone to her purse and contemplated the possibility she'd have to jump out the next time the driver stopped at an intersection. She should've known letting the desk clerk call a cab for her was a mistake. What if he was in cahoots with Officer Benson?

As the driver slowed to take the corner, she clasped the door handle.

"The next street on your right will take you back to the street I want," Laura said, still holding the handle in case the driver had other plans. She prayed Beth was home. Laura hadn't known where else to go after the police released her. They wouldn't tell her when or if Garrett was being released, and she hadn't wanted to worry his mother before he had a chance to speak to her. She'd texted him, hoping he'd soon see it.

She flinched when her phone beeped with an incoming text. But she didn't dare take her hand off the door handle now to see if it was from Garrett.

The driver steered onto the street as instructed.

Laura expelled the breath she'd been holding. "You can drop me at the next corner." If the man was in cahoots with Benson, it was bad enough he knew what street she was headed for, never mind giving away the house number.

The driver flicked on his signal and coasted through the intersection.

"This is good," Laura said. "Stop here."

The driver stomped on the brakes.

Laura tossed twenty dollars onto the front seat. "Keep the change." She bolted from the car and slammed the door, then hurried across the stranger's yard.

The cab seemed to sit there forever. Was the driver watching to see which house she entered?

Another car rounded the corner and came up behind him, honking its horn.

The cab finally moved on.

Laura crouched behind a hedge until she saw the cab disappear, then sprinted across the street to Beth's house and pounded on the front door.

Beth opened the door. "Laura?"

"Let me in." Laura rushed past her. "Shut the door. Turn off the front light."

Beth closed the door, slid the dead bolt into place, and flipped the switch for the porch light. "What's going on?"

Laura shook her head, second-guessing her decision to come here. What if she was endangering Beth?

"You're shaking." Beth wrapped an arm around Laura's shoulders and guided her into the kitchen, where she put on the kettle.

Remembering Garrett's call, Laura scrolled through her text messages to see if he'd responded to her text. Nothing. "What should I do?" she lamented to Beth. "They've got Caroline, but I don't know who they are. And I can't trust the police."

"What are you talking about?"

Laura related the events of the past few hours, not sure she was making any sense.

"I don't see anything you can do," Beth said. "You know they won't stop at shooting whoever gets in their way."

Laura sank onto a kitchen chair and leaned over the table, resting her head in her hands. "Garrett will know what to do. Maybe he can enlist some of his old army buddies to help us track her down."

"Have you forgotten that PrimeCorp supplies the army with munitions?" Beth set a steaming cup of tea on the table in front of Laura along with a plate of cookies. "They might not be too eager to take the company down."

"Good point." Her phone beeped a text alert, and Laura snatched it up. "Garrett says he got my message and is on his way. His lawyer is driving him to the impound now to get his car."

Forty-five minutes later, Laura paced the living room. "He should've been here by now."

"He'll be here," Beth insisted.

"What if they sabotaged his car?"

Beth called her fiancé. "Have there been any reports of traffic accidents, a car going off the road, exploding, anything like that in the last hour?"

Laura could hear Ryan's laughter on the other end of the connection. "No, it's been a quiet day. We haven't been called out once."

"Have you been listening to the police scanner like I asked?"

"Yeah, nothing's gone down since the shooting at the lake."

After thanking him and reminding him how much she loved him, Beth clicked off. "I think we can rule out sabotage. He probably got lost. Or maybe had car trouble."

Laura's phone rang. She checked the screen. "It's his mother. What do I do?"

"Answer it."

"Oh, I'm glad I reached you," Nancy said. "Garrett's not answering his phone. I was wondering when you planned to be home. It's getting late."

"I'm sorry. We should've called sooner. We had a lead we needed to follow." Laura paused, hating to keep things from the woman, but she didn't want to worry her unduly either. "I'm afraid we'll be a while yet. I feel terrible about taking all of Garrett's time these past few days."

"Nonsense. I haven't seen him this vibrant in months. He's always been a problem solver. Being able to help you has done him a world of good."

Laura bit her lip, certain Nancy wouldn't be saying so if she knew the whole story. "I'll have him call you as soon as we figure out what we're going to do."

Knocking erupted at the front door.

Laura ran for it, realizing as she grabbed the door handle that she'd hung up on Garrett's mom without saying goodbye. Coming to her senses, she stopped short of throwing the door open and peeked through the peephole instead.

At the sight of Garrett standing outside the door, sound and whole, every muscle in her body felt like wet noodles. She opened the door. "What took you so long? I was afraid something happened to you."

The amusement in Garrett's eyes warmed her to the tips of her toes. "I'm happy to see you too. May I come in?"

Stepping back, she opened the door wider.

He nodded at Beth. "Sorry about the delay. My lawyer had to drive me to the impound to pick up my car, which took twice as long as it should have because of a construction detour. Then I was halfway here before I realized I'd left my phone charging in his car, and I had to hunt him down to retrieve it."

"She was afraid the bad guys sabotaged your car," Beth told him.

Laura glared at her.

"What?" Beth asked. "You were."

"When I didn't see you at the police station after they released me, I was petrified Officer Benson had decided to make you disappear too," Garrett admitted.

Laura blinked back tears. "Do you think that's what they've done to Caroline? Made her disappear—permanently?"

Garrett clasped her hands. "I'm sorry. I shouldn't have said that. We're not going to give up. Okay?"

Laura nodded. "The senator's doing all she can too. She's the one who orchestrated our release."

Garrett furrowed his brow. "How did she know we'd been arrested?"

"I used my phone call to contact her and explained everything. She must've lit a fire under the officers to get on with testing the gun and our clothes for residues, because within half an hour of my call, they let me go."

"Did you mention your suspicions about the cop with the tattoo?" Garrett asked.

Laura stifled a shiver. "No, I figured I'd be safer if he didn't know I could identify him."

"Good thinking." Garrett sipped the tea Beth handed him. "I've been trying to figure out how Caroline's presumed captor found her at Dwayne's cottage."

"The cops have known since church let out that Brian Schumacher traded her an SUV for her car," Beth reminded him. "The police could've spotted it by the lake."

"Dwayne's cabin isn't exactly on a regular patrol route," Garrett said.

"No, but if the people after her heard she had a boyfriend, they might've concluded she'd hide at his place," Laura said.

"But Dwayne was an ex-boyfriend," Garrett pointed out.

"Maybe they didn't know that," Laura said.

Garrett frowned. "At this point, I guess it's the only angle we've got. So, who knew about Caroline's ex?"

"Her friend at the newspaper," Laura replied. "I kind of doubt Caroline told her colleagues at work. She's pretty private about things like that."

"Mel knew," Garrett reminded her. "And he knew about the cottage."

"Mel's not a dirty cop," Laura insisted. He couldn't have changed that much since high school.

"I knew," Beth chimed in. "But I didn't tell anyone. Not even my fiancé."

"I told the senator and Lieutenant Reynolds when they found us in the woods," Laura said.

"Also Brian Schumacher and my mom," Garrett added.

"Oh, you're supposed to call your mom." Laura filled him in on how much she'd already told her.

Garrett took a few minutes to check in with his mother, then returned to Laura with a fresh barrage of questions. "How did the senator respond to your call from the police station?"

"She asked all kinds of questions about what Dwayne had said. She was clearly concerned about what Caroline's abductors want from her. It makes me wonder what other projects Caroline might've been working on besides her investigation on PrimeCorp."

"Was the senator asking out of concern for stopping an information breach or something else?"

"Something else?" Laura asked.

"You didn't tell her your suspicion about at least one of the cops," Garrett reminded her.

"That's because I didn't want Officer Benson to conclude I'd become a liability."

"I understand that," Garrett acknowledged. "And I'm glad you didn't. Because there is another possibility—the cops could be working for her."

"Caroline said not to trust anyone,'" Beth reminded them. "If she trusted a woman as powerful as the senator, surely your cousin would've gone to her in the first place."

"We already know PrimeCorp's CEO is a heavy contributor to advancing the senator's presidential bid," Garrett said. "He might even be the one with a cop or two on his payroll."

Laura clasped her hands to stop their trembling. "So, you think the senator has Caroline?"

"No," Garrett answered.

Laura frowned. "But you just said—"

"I know, but if Senator Funk already had her, why did she ask you so many questions?"

"Maybe because she wanted to ensure Laura hasn't uncovered the same secret Caroline did," Beth theorized.

Garrett nodded, seeming to mull over the possibility. "Or maybe there's another player involved in all of this."

"Didn't you think Doc's death was somehow connected to PrimeCorp?" Beth asked.

Garrett snapped his fingers. "That reminds me. I asked an old friend who's now a state trooper if he could find out the name of the owner of the truck that struck Uncle Richard." He tapped the name of a contact on his phone and held it to his ear. A moment later, he clicked it off. "Went to voice mail."

His phone rang.

He answered it without reading the screen. "Joel?"

"Did you see it?" His mother's voice vibrated from the phone loud enough for them all to hear.

"See what?" Garrett asked. "What are you talking about?"

"The channel 12 news."

Beth switched on the TV.

The news anchor was reporting that Officer Joel Layton had been shot in the line of duty and was fighting for his life.

Garrett's face paled. He sank onto the sofa.

The phone slipped from his hand to the floor, and his mother could be heard saying, "I'm sorry."

Laura picked up the phone. "This is Laura. Can Garrett call you back later? He's pretty shaken up."

"Of course," Nancy said. "Maybe I shouldn't have called, but Garrett was talking to poor Joel yesterday. I thought he'd want to know."

Laura's throat constricted, recalling what the hardware store owner intimated happened to anyone who looked into PrimeCorp's dirty little secrets. "This is the same Joel that Garrett asked to investigate the owner of the truck that struck Doc?"

"That's right."

Laura thanked her and hung up, then motioned to Beth to shut off the TV.

Garrett rested his elbows on his knees and clutched his head in his hands.

As Laura set down Garrett's phone, she realized he had three new voice mails. One was from his mother, one from her, and one from Joel Layton.

Laura dropped to one knee in front of Garrett and gently pressed the phone into his hands. "Your friend left you a voice mail."

Garrett stared at the phone before clicking on the message.

"I got the info you wanted," a cheerful baritone said. "The truck owner's name is Ralph Henry. And his alibi is ironclad. The guy was in the hospital having gastrointestinal bypass surgery at the time his truck was stolen. His sister noticed the truck missing from his driveway and called it in."

Laura sighed. *Another dead end.*

Laura caught a ride home that night with Garrett, but she insisted it was time she resumed sleeping at her own house. Surprisingly, Garrett didn't put up as much of a protest as she'd expected. Not that she was disappointed or anything.

He did search her house from top to bottom and checked the locks on the windows and doors. "Keep the phone near you at all times. Is it charged?"

She nodded.

"Good. If you hear anything out of the ordinary, call me."

"Are you trying to ruin my night's sleep?"

He arched a brow. "Turnabout's fair play, isn't it?"

"What?"

"You're ruining my sleep by insisting on returning home," Garrett said. "I'll be running to the window at every sound to ensure you don't have any trouble." The teasing spark in his tone was tempered by his wary expression.

Touched by his concern, Laura squeezed his arm.

His muscles jumped beneath her fingers, and he froze where he stood. His blue eyes bored into hers.

She swallowed in an effort to moisten her drying throat, then hitched her thumb over her shoulder. "I should go to bed now. I have to take my mom to the hospital in the morning."

"Who's taking care of the diner?" Garrett asked, making no move to leave.

"One of my part-timers. Well, good night," Laura said. Realizing she still held his arm, she abruptly dropped her hand and opened the front door for him.

"Be sure to lock this," he said before leaving.

She closed the door behind him and immediately set the dead bolt.

Expelling a breath, she leaned back against the door and tried to calm down. *What I need is some warm milk to help me sleep.* She went to the kitchen and poured herself a glass, then put it in the microwave. After going full tilt all day, every inch of her oozed exhaustion, but her mind was still racing, replaying every minute detail of the recent events.

Laura sipped the warm milk. A long soak in the bathtub would be nice. Then again, the thought of being so vulnerable if someone broke in made her feel uneasy. Instead, she finished her milk, got into her cozy pajamas, and took a book to bed.

Two hours later, she was halfway through the book and couldn't recall a single word. This was crazy. Most nights she fell asleep before she managed to get through one chapter. She padded to the kitchen for a glass of water and glanced out the window at Garrett's house. The lights were all out.

So much for me keeping him up all night.

After setting her empty glass in the sink, Laura opened her laptop. If she wasn't going to sleep, she might as well do something useful. She'd been thinking about Garrett's friend being shot. Was it really a coincidence, or might it have something to do with his DMV database activity earlier that day? She wanted to believe it was unrelated, because if the bad guys saw his snooping as a threat, then she definitely wasn't safe. Never mind that they already had Caroline.

Laura opened her browser and typed in *Ralph Henry.*

Earlier, surrounded by both Garrett and Beth, it had seemed pretty clear the man with his ironclad alibi was a bona fide dead end. But by half past one in the morning, the lines had grown fuzzy.

She scrolled through the social media pages of various Ralph Henrys, hoping something would pop out at her. Here was a page for Ralph H. with a post of a picture of a truck identical to the one that struck Doc. She scrutinized all the posts on the guy's page for the past three months. She was about to give up when she came to a collection of pictures from the guy's birthday party. *Bingo.*

One of the pictures depicted a blond heartthrob identical to the driver she'd seen run down Doc. She peeked out the window toward Garrett's house, hoping a light had clicked on since the last time she'd looked.

No such luck.

Laura printed the image and hunted for the guy's name, first in the photo section to see if he'd been tagged and then amongst the pictures of Henry's friends. There was no mention of him anywhere.

She shut down her computer, collected the picture of the guy from her printer, and returned to bed. Staring at the picture, she murmured, "You're going to pay for what you did. I may not know who you are now. But I'll find out very soon."

After Laura clicked off the light, she contemplated her options. She'd recently read an article about how some police departments scanned the Internet using a new facial recognition software to ID suspects. Unlike the FBI's recognition software that only used criminal databases, this software searched likenesses on social media sites where photos of people abounded and were often tagged, allowing the names to be cross-referenced to dig up addresses.

She wasn't sure if their local department used the new software. But maybe Mel could do something with the picture through his Pittsburgh station's resources.

Of course, they could pay Ralph Henry a visit and ask him the man's identity. He might be very interested to learn that his party guest had stolen his truck.

Or she could return to Douglas's hardware store to see if he recognized the man. Perhaps he worked for PrimeCorp. Douglas might be the kind of guy who would recognize all the bad apples in the company on sight.

At some point Laura drifted off to sleep, because when a dog's bark startled her awake, the sun was already up. Was Garrett? She squinted at the clock. It was 7:47. She never slept this late.

Laura phoned the diner to make sure her part-timer was managing okay.

Her cook, Tom, answered. "She's doing fine. Say hi to your mother for me."

"I will." Thinking of Tom's tattoos, she said, "Maybe you can tell me something. How common is it for a guy to have a tattoo on the inside of his arm?"

"Not uncommon. Why?"

"Remember I told you about my intruder Friday night? Yesterday I remembered that he had a tattoo on the inside of his wrist. I didn't see the whole thing. But it had sweeping lines like a decorative script."

"Since the wearer sees it all the time, a wrist tattoo usually has special meaning. It might remind him of a loved one or his faith."

"The man clobbered me," Laura said. "I don't think it'd be his religious convictions."

"Was it a person's name?"

"No." She squinted, trying to reconstruct the image in her mind. "I got the impression it was a foreign word. Possibly Latin. It was written upside down."

"Interesting. Tattoos are usually drawn so others see them right side up, but maybe it was more important to this guy that the words be for him to read."

"I think the first word might've been '*carpe.*' Have you ever seen anyone with a tattoo like that?"

"Sure. *Carpe diem* means 'seize the day.' I usually wouldn't associate it with a criminal type. Then again, criminals are more likely to go after what they want now, never mind the consequences."

After thanking him, Laura ended the conversation and made quick work of getting ready to go, so she'd have time to fill Garrett in on the picture she'd found before driving her mom to the hospital. Grabbing a granola bar to go, she caught Garrett leaving his house.

The shadows beneath his eyes told her that he hadn't slept any better than she had, but the concern creasing his forehead eased when his gaze met hers. "I was coming over to check on you. Did you sleep okay?"

"No, but it's a good thing, because I found this on Ralph H.'s social media page." She showed him the picture she'd printed. "This is the guy who ran down your uncle."

Garrett gaped at her. "You're sure?"

"Positive. Well, almost positive. The trouble is I couldn't find his name online. I thought we might pay Ralph Henry a visit and ask him."

Garrett held up his hands. "No way. Definitely not a good idea. We don't want this guy to know you can identify him. We should give the picture to Lieutenant Reynolds."

"Are you kidding me? I'm not taking this to the local cops. What if this guy has Caroline?"

"Then what about asking your friend with the Pittsburgh police?"

Laura waffled. She was pretty sure she could trust Mel, but she still didn't like that the bad guys just happened to catch Caroline at Dwayne's cabin shortly after Mel had told Laura about it.

Her phone rang. "This is probably my mom, making sure I haven't forgotten about—" Laura stopped when she checked the screen. It was a private number.

"Who is it?" Garrett asked.

"I don't know." Most of the time she'd ignore a number she didn't have in her contact list, but what if it was Caroline trying to reach her? She connected. "Hello?"

"Oh, I'm so glad I finally reached you," Caroline said. "I stopped by Friday night, but you were out."

"What's going on?" Laura asked. "I've been worried sick about you. Are you all right?"

"Why wouldn't I be?"

Seriously? Was she really not going to talk about what happened— the intruder, selling her car, her dead ex-boyfriend? "Dwayne's dead. Did you know that?"

"What?" Caroline must've covered the phone, because whatever she said next sounded distant and muffled. Her next words to Laura were shaky. "It's my fault. I never should've involved him."

"Involved him in what?" Laura tapped the icon for speakerphone so Garrett could hear her reply too.

Caroline's exhalation sounded as rattled as her voice. "Someone was following me, and I didn't know who, so I figured I'd leave town for the weekend and visit you. But somehow the guy tracked me there. He must've had a transmitter attached to my car or was monitoring the GPS in my phone or something. So, I ditched the car and my phone and went to Dwayne's. I figured my ex-boyfriend's house was the last place anyone would look for me."

Laura quirked an eyebrow at Garrett for nailing that one. "But they did. Who was it? How did you get away?"

Once again Caroline seemed to muffle the phone a moment before continuing. "It turns out it wasn't me they were after. Dwayne was in deep with the mob, and the people following me actually wanted him. I ended up leading them right to him."

"Why did they ransack your apartment?" Laura asked. "Dwayne said the shooter took you."

"You talked to Dwayne?" Caroline's voice broke. "His assailant didn't take me. It was more like I was told if I knew what was good for me, I'd leave."

Laura scrunched her forehead against the pain pulsating through her thoughts. The whole thing didn't add up. They had to know Caroline would be a liability to them. She may not have seen them shoot Dwayne, but surely she could identify his assailants on sight. Was she being so cryptic because she feared the phone was bugged?

"Does Senator Funk know you're home?" Laura asked. The senator could ensure Caroline got the protection she needed—unless she was somehow part of all this. "I was supposed to tell the senator when I heard from you. She was concerned about you and kind about helping me."

"I always told you she was very caring."

Laura frowned. Caroline had never described the senator as caring. *Bulldog* was the most memorable descriptor she'd used.

"I'm sorry," Caroline continued. "I would've called sooner. Honestly, I didn't know you'd realize I'd been at your house."

Laura didn't believe that for a moment. A man had followed Caroline into the house, but Laura bit her lip rather than point out the obvious. She wanted to ask about PrimeCorp, what Caroline knew about Doc's investigation into the company, and why someone had ransacked Caroline's apartment—a question she'd neatly skirted.

"Listen, I've got to go," Caroline said. "We'll do lunch soon." The connection went dead.

Laura stared at her phone.

Garrett brightened. "That's one less thing to worry about."

"Uh, no."

"What do you mean? She said she was fine."

"No. When I asked her if she was okay, she replied with why wouldn't she be."

"Which means she's fine."

"She said 'honestly,' which she's told me time and again people only say when they're hedging or outright lying. She's trying to send me a message."

Garrett shook his head. "Plenty of people use it to mean exactly what it says."

"Not Caroline," she replied. "Besides, she said that she *honestly* didn't know I'd realize she'd been at the house when she'd left a note for me in the novel on my bedside table."

"Good point. She could've been trying to alert you to the possibility your phone was tapped."

"That's what I'd first assumed." Laura considered other possibilities. "She claimed the mob guy let her leave, but her SUV was still in the driveway."

"But Dwayne's car wasn't. She could've taken it."

"Or Caroline was taken, and her captors forced her to make the call to get us to back off."

Laura's phone beeped the reminder alarm she'd set to leave to pick up her mother. "I've got to go," Laura said to Garrett, tamping down the impulse to invite him along. He didn't have time to play bodyguard 24-7.

Nancy hurried out of the house. "Your aunt is on the phone. She needs you to come into the office to see today's patients. The locum called in sick."

Garrett took the phone from his mother.

"Garrett said you're taking your mother to the hospital today," Nancy said to Laura. "Would you care for some company? I'd like to meet her."

Nancy's eager entreaty and bright voice eased Laura's anxiety over Caroline's call. "I'm sure Mom would love that."

"Let me grab my purse and sweater," Nancy said, then returned to the house.

Garrett pocketed his phone. "I'll be tied up until at least three. Promise me you won't do anything dangerous on your own, like visit Ralph Henry." The concern in his gaze tempered his stern tone. "Later we can sit down together and figure out what's really going on with Caroline."

Laura's insides churned. Her mom's appointment would keep her busy for the next couple of hours, but a lot could happen between now and three in the afternoon. "I was thinking I could try calling Caroline at her office on the pretense of planning a party for our aunt. That way at least we'd know if she's in the office without anyone suspecting I was checking up on her."

"Or maybe your mom could place the call to make it even less suspicious," he suggested.

"I'll see. I don't want to have to answer too many questions before we know how Caroline really is."

Nancy bustled out of the house. "I'm ready." She kissed Garrett on the cheek. "I'm off with Laura. I'll see you later."

"Be good," Garrett said to his mother.

At first, Laura thought Garrett might've asked his mom to invite herself in order to keep an eye on Laura, but his warning suggested that he feared his mom had her own reasons for wanting to come along. Laura smothered a giggle. It was kind of cute having a mother championing her to her son. But from Garrett's reaction, she doubted she had to worry about anything coming of it. Her chest squeezed. *Terrific.* Apparently, her heart and her head weren't on the same wavelength.

During the short drive to her mother's house, Laura filled Nancy in on a bit more family history, grateful to have something to distract her from her worries about Caroline.

When Laura's mother joined them, she and Nancy chattered away as if they'd known each other all their lives.

Since Laura couldn't get a parking spot near the hospital entrance, she dropped the pair at the door and told them she'd catch up to them in the waiting room on the second floor, where her mom had to sign in.

Laura circled the parking lot twice before locating an empty spot at the far end. The air was already hot and muggy, so rather than walk around the building to the front entrance, she went in a side door and promptly got lost searching for elevators to take her to the second floor. Rounding the corner, she spotted them as a doctor in a white lab coat stepped into one.

"Hold the elevator!" Laura rushed toward it and gasped when she recognized the doctor inside.

Dr. Henri's eyes widened. She quickly tapped a button, and the elevator door closed before Laura could get inside.

What was Dr. Henri doing here? Laura pressed the button to call the elevator back and stared at the numbers over the door. It went to the third floor before the numbers descended once more. Laura pulled out her phone and called Garrett.

The phone rang once, twice. The empty elevator returned, and Laura stepped on. "Please answer."

"What's going on? Is everything okay?" Garrett sounded out of breath, as if he'd run for the phone.

Laura pressed the button for the third floor, certain Nancy would keep her mother occupied while she waited for her appointment. "Your locum is here at the hospital. Only she isn't sick. In fact, she seemed unnerved that I'd seen her. She's wearing a lab coat and a stethoscope."

"What?" Garrett's voice pitched higher than she'd ever heard it.

"Does she have hospital privileges here?" Laura asked. The elevator stopped at the third floor, and she exited it. Dr. Henri wasn't in sight. Laura went to the nurses' station to ask if anyone had seen her.

Garrett groaned. "This can't be good."

"What are you thinking?"

"What if Ralph Henry is really Ralph Henri—Henry pronounced with a French accent?"

Laura's breath stalled in her throat. "You think she's Ralph Henry's sister? The one who reported the car stolen?"

"Maybe. If she's mixed up in this, it would explain why she magically volunteered to fill in as locum until my aunt sold the practice."

"But why is she here at the hospital?" Laura asked Garrett. To the nurse at the nurses' station, Laura said, "Did you see which way the female doctor who just got off the elevator went?"

"Room 321."

"What are you doing?" Garrett asked. "Don't confront her."

"We need to know what she's up to." When Laura reached room 321, she spotted Dr. Henri sticking a needle into the patient's IV. "What are you doing?"

The woman's gaze snapped to Laura, then drifted over her shoulder.

Laura spun around and saw the face that would forever be seared on her brain. "It's you."

"What's going on?" Garrett yelled into the phone.

A faint male voice said gently, "Now what are you doing out of your room?"

Laura's shriek followed by the clatter of her phone falling to the floor sent Garrett racing from his office. "I've got an emergency!" he shouted to his aunt as he passed the reception desk. "Cancel the rest of my appointments."

He kept the phone pressed to his ear as he climbed into his car. But all he could hear was scuffling. He careened out of the parking lot to angry honks. Then an alarm sounded from Laura's phone, followed by a PA announcement. "Code blue. We have a code blue in room 321."

Dread crept into Garrett's stomach. Code blue meant a medical emergency. Who had Laura—and what had they done to her?

The connection went dead. Garrett swerved onto the next street. "Call Mom," he ordered his phone.

His mom picked up on the second ring.

"Is Laura with you?" Garrett asked.

"No, she's parking the car. What's wrong? You sound as if you're out of breath."

"Listen carefully. Laura called me from inside the hospital. I think she saw Uncle Richard's killer." The words jammed in his throat, but he forced them out. "I think he took her. You need to do whatever you can to lock the hospital down. Tell them a child's been abducted if you have to. I'm on my way."

"What are you talking about?"

"There's no time to explain. Go to the nurses' station, and tell them to get security to lock down the hospital." Garrett clicked off before his mother could ask any more questions and tried Laura's number again.

A man answered.

"Where's Laura?" Garrett heard what sounded like a distant car horn, then the slam of a car door. *Her abductor already has her out of the hospital.*

"If you want to see her alive, go alone to where it all began. Don't tell the cops."

"Where's that? Wait!"

The connection ended.

Garrett screeched to a stop at a red light and pounded the steering wheel. What was he supposed to do? He was two blocks from the hospital. But the guy already had Laura in a vehicle, and Garrett had no idea what the guy meant.

If you want to see her alive ...

The words rang in his ears.

A blue sports car pulled up in the lane beside him and revved its engine.

Richard's accident. It started with the accident.

The light turned green. Garrett headed back to Main Street. He pulled to the curb outside the diner, jumped out of his car, and scanned the street. Laura wasn't there. He crossed the street to the exact spot where his uncle had been struck and almost got clipped himself.

A driver blared his horn.

Beth came out of the diner. "Are you okay?"

He ran back across the street. "Have you seen Laura?"

"No, she had to take her mother to the hospital this morning, remember?"

"Yeah, but he got to her."

"Who got to her?"

"The guy who killed my uncle." *I think.* Garrett didn't have time for explanations. "He told me if I want to find her alive, I have to go to where it all began."

"The cemetery?" Beth suggested.

"Yes." Garrett jumped into his car and took off toward the cemetery.

His mother called. "I couldn't get security to lock down the hospital. A nurse on the third floor recalled Laura asking after a doctor and directed her to a room in which the patient coded a few minutes later."

"Laura wasn't there?"

"No, and they want to question her about it. They're going over the security feeds on the exits to see if she left. They seem to think she might have done something."

"It wasn't her."

"I know. But the patient—it was your friend Joel."

Garrett felt sucker punched. "Did he make it?"

"Yes, they saved him."

Relief swept over him, but it was quickly overwhelmed by a fresh wave of panic. If they'd kill a police officer for looking up a file, it could already be too late for Laura. He veered into the cemetery. "I've got to go. I think I might know where they took her."

The instant he clicked off, his phone rang again.

Garrett slammed on his brakes near his uncle's burial plot and snatched up the phone.

"Ticktock, Dr. Simons."

"I don't know where I'm supposed to go."

"That's a shame, Doc."

"I want to speak to her. How do I know you even have her?"

"Garrett?" Laura's quavering voice lit his veins on fire.

"Are you okay? Have they hurt you? Where are you?"

The man's voice boomed once more. "You have ten minutes."

"Don't come!" Laura screamed in the background. "It's a trap!"

"You won't get away with this," Laura warned her captor from the back seat of his darkly tinted sports car—too expensive for a hired henchman.

"I already have."

"The cops know I was searching for you and my cousin. And not only the dirty cops your boss is paying to cover up for you. Honest cops who uphold the law."

He laughed. "My boss, huh? You clearly don't even know who I am."

"Yes I do. You're the creep who ran Doc down in cold blood."

They were heading south out of town—where it all began. PrimeCorp's dump site? Where Doc had taken the pictures.

"I discovered the pictures Doc took of your boss's dump site. The cops have them," she lied, not sure if it would help her cause or put more officers at risk. "Dr. Henri was too late with that honest cop she tried to kill. He'd already told us Ralph Henry owned the truck you used to run down Doc. And I found your picture on his social media page. The cops have that too."

Laura flicked her gaze to Dr. Henri, sitting in the passenger seat. "I suppose Ralph is your brother and you decided to lend your boyfriend his truck to do his dirty work before you conveniently reported it stolen?"

Her startled glance to Laura's captor confirmed she'd guessed right.

"For your information, I didn't borrow the truck with the intention of hurting anyone," the man hissed. "I borrowed it because it had four-wheel drive and could handle the lousy dirt road into the dump site. The dump site I'd been about to have cleaned up."

"Why is that?" Laura asked. "You got a sudden case of guilt over the people who were getting sick because of it? Or because you were worried Doc was about to expose your company?"

"Yes, if you must know."

Wait a minute. *He'd* been about to have the site cleaned up? Not his boss? Laura blinked. The expensive sports car with leather seats suddenly made sense.

"Brad," Dr. Henri hissed from the passenger seat, "you shouldn't be telling her this."

Laura's throat constricted. Brad? As in Brad Carruthers, the son of PrimeCorp's owner?

Brad snorted. "Why? She won't be alive to talk about it."

Laura winced.

He smirked at Laura in the rearview mirror. "If you want the whole sordid truth, my father thinks I'm useless, not fit to run his company. So, when word of the uptick in health problems in the area came to our attention, I decided to prove my mettle to Dad. I drove to the abandoned site to assess the situation and plan a cleanup before anything could be definitively linked to our company."

"How noble of you," Laura said sarcastically.

"That's when I found your doc snooping around, taking pictures. I followed him to town, planning to reason with him, maybe bribe him." Brad shrugged. "But when that kid pulled up beside me in his souped-up car—well, let's just say I recognized a better opportunity when I saw one."

Laura cringed.

"Afterward we decided it was better to ditch the truck in a sketchy neighborhood and claim it was stolen," Brad continued. "It was a stroke of luck that a criminal there decided to steal it for real and take it off the road."

"But you didn't count on me being unwilling to be bullied by your cop friend into identifying the driver as the same man I saw run down Doc," Laura said.

Brad chuckled. "I suspect the cops had their own reasons for bullying you. Like quickly closing a high-profile case all neat and tidy." He steered into the woods.

The terrain suddenly got so bumpy it seemed to rattle Laura's bones.

He braked and shoved the car into park. "I'm afraid you'll have to walk from here."

"Killing me is not going to make this go away," Laura said. She wanted to say lots of people knew what he'd done, but she was petrified he'd demand names so he could go out and kill them all.

"Now you'll never know, will you?"

"Wait." Laura braced her foot into the floorboard so he couldn't haul her out of the car. "Other people know."

Brad yanked her from the back seat and shoved her ahead of him along the overgrown road. "That's where you're wrong. My doctor friend back there has spent the last six weeks meeting patients and searching files. Nowhere and with no one did your doc share his theory about PrimeCorp's connection to the increase in medical conditions in his patients from south of town."

"If she was so sure, why did you have all the computers stolen from the office?" Laura asked. "Why did you break into my diner? My house? Why try to run me down outside Caroline's apartment?"

"Insurance. My assistant confirmed at the cemetery that the doctor hadn't passed his phone with the photos to you. So it wasn't until you balked at ID'ing the driver found in the truck that I decided to keep a closer eye on you. When the senator's office alerted me that her aide, your cousin, was asking questions about PrimeCorp, I realized I'd have to take more drastic measures."

Laura stumbled. "Does the senator know what you're doing?"

Brad hauled Laura back onto her feet and continued to shove her forward. "She's not naive."

They trudged on in silence, Laura's mind racing to find a means of escape.

"This is about right." Brad drew her to an abrupt halt. "Where it all began." He pushed her to her knees and stooped toward a bush where he'd apparently hidden something.

Laura surged to her feet and ran. But her hands were still tied behind her back, making it nearly impossible to keep her balance.

She hadn't made it more than thirty yards before he caught her, this time with a heavy rope slung over his shoulder. She screamed.

Brad slapped one hand over her mouth and walked her back to the location he'd chosen, then tied her to a tree.

She screamed again.

This time Brad shoved a cloth into her mouth, then bound her legs for good measure. He pulled a gas can from the bush. He splashed the gasoline in a wide circle around her, avoiding the trail they'd walked on. "We have to give your boyfriend a fighting chance," he said by way of explanation, "or he won't risk his life to save you, will he?"

She shuddered at the thought of how Brad expected them both to die.

His cell phone rang. "What is it?"

"What's taking you so long?" Dr. Henri's shrill voice demanded. "We have to get out of here."

"On my way." Brad pocketed his phone and made a show of lighting a long wooden match, a sick smile curving his lips.

The man was crazy.

"Perfect, isn't it?" Brad gazed lovingly at the flame. "Fire is the ultimate purifier. After it sweeps through the forest, any evidence this ever had anything to do with PrimeCorp will be vaporized." He snatched the cloth from her mouth, exited the circle of gasoline, and flicked the match to the ground.

The fuel swooshed into flames.

"Where it all began," Garrett mumbled. "With the patients?" But he'd been at the office when Laura called. Besides, it was too public.

Public. Of course. How had he not realized sooner? The guy would want to lure them somewhere out of the way. Where it all began. It began with what had caused so many patients' symptoms—the dump site.

The town's fire siren wailed, and trucks blasted by, heading south.

Garrett raced after them. He smelled the smoke first and felt physically sick. *It can't be too late. I can't be too late. Lord, please show me a way to get to Laura.*

Despair filled him at the sight of the forest ablaze.

He pulled to the side of the road behind a row of vehicles of every description. Volunteer firefighters jumped out and raced to the rigs to join the effort.

I can't be too late. Surely her captor wanted Garrett to perish with Laura. He'd have expected Garrett to be able to get to her before the fire reached her. *The back road.*

He did a U-turn and searched for the junction of the trail to the road. Had he passed it already? He squinted at the trees, trying to make out something familiar. He slammed on his brakes and lurched from the car.

A four-wheeler barreling his way narrowly missed him as he ran across the road.

The driver slowed and came back around. "Where are you going?"

Recognizing Matt from his aunt's house, Garrett asked, "Can I borrow that four-wheeler?"

"My dad told me to bring it here for the firefighters."

"I think Laura is in the forest. Down this trail."

Matt revved his engine and pulled onto the trail. "Get on."

"I can't ask you to go in there," Garrett said. "It's too dangerous."

"You didn't ask. I volunteered. Now get on."

Garrett was barely seated before Matt took off like a madman.

Rising a foot or more off his seat with each bump they hit, Garrett held on for dear life. The smoke grew so thick he could scarcely breathe. His eyes stung. The air was getting hotter. Too hot.

Matt slowed, and as the engine quieted, Garrett heard something.

Garrett motioned for Matt to cut the engine. "Listen."

A faint, hoarse cry came from straight ahead of them.

"It's Laura. Keep driving." For some reason the flames seemed to be eating their way through the forest away from the road instead of closing in on it.

"I can't get much closer!" Matt yelled over the increasing roar of the inferno.

"Okay, wait here for me."

"You're going in there?"

"I won't lose her as long as I have breath left." Garrett coughed, the smoke strangling his lungs. He would have given anything for a medical mask.

Matt slapped a pocketknife into Garrett's hand. "Take this. You might need it."

Garrett raced down the trail. When he reached the wall of moving flames on either side, he held his breath and surged between them. And just like that, it was eerily still, as if he were in the eye of a storm. "Laura!"

"Here. I'm over—" Coughing cut off her words.

He squinted through the smoke and saw her struggling with the ropes that held her. He skidded to his knees at her side and opened Matt's knife.

"It was Brad Carruthers, the son of PrimeCorp's owner." She coughed.

"Tell me when we're safe." Garrett sliced the ropes binding her hands behind her back, then went to work on the thicker ones used to tie her to the tree.

"Dr. Henri is his girlfriend."

"Let's focus on getting you out of here."

Tears streamed down her cheeks. "You shouldn't have come." Laura wriggled her legs out of the bottom ropes.

He hacked through the ropes around her torso, then urged her forward.

Her legs instantly buckled.

"Can you walk?"

"My legs are numb."

Garrett wrapped his arm around her waist and helped her down the trail. "Matt has a four-wheeler up ahead."

Laura slumped to the ground.

"Stay with me," he begged. "You have to stay with me. I can't be the reason another person dies."

The hum of Matt's motor broke through the roar in Garrett's head.

Powered by a surge of adrenaline, he scooped Laura into his arms and stumbled on.

A loud crack cut the air. A burning branch crashed to the ground, glancing off Garrett's shoulder and leaving searing pain behind it. He fell forward, covering Laura as best he could to protect her from the flames.

Matt raced toward them and threw a tarp over Garrett's back, smothering the flames. "Come on." He hauled Garrett to his feet.

Laura roused a little, mumbling but not opening her eyes.

Matt helped Garrett get her to the four-wheeler. "You'll have to hold her on your lap."

Garrett nodded. He didn't plan on letting go of her anytime soon. Not until the creep who did this was behind bars.

"Hang on!" the teen shouted and gunned the gas.

"We're going home," Garrett whispered in Laura's ear. "Hang on." With each jolt of the vehicle, fresh pain sliced through his body from where the burning branch had clipped him. He gritted his teeth against it and focused on trying to rouse Laura once more. She'd been breathing in smoke for a lot longer than he had, and he could already feel what it was doing to him. Her carbon monoxide levels could already be dangerously high.

Laura's eyes remained closed.

"Wake up for me. You can't leave me now. Not when we're so close to getting out of here. Not when I haven't told you how I feel about you." His voice cracked. Garrett knew he was babbling, but he didn't care. "You've got to know I've been kind of holding back my feelings for you these past few days."

Was it his imagination, or did she snuggle against him a little more?

He gently swept the hair from her face, his fingers tingling at the warmth of her skin. She was so beautiful. "I want to see what the future might hold for us. Please hang on so we can have that chance."

Laura struggled to open her eyes as the four-wheeler came to an abrupt stop.

"We need paramedics here!" Matt shouted. "They were in the fire."

Garrett still held her close, but his expression was etched with pain.

"We made it," she said, her voice scarcely more than a whisper.

He didn't respond. His arms went slack.

Her pulse quickened. "Are you okay?"

Two paramedics lifted her from his lap and put her on a gurney.

"Garrett!" Laura twisted to keep him in view.

Garrett's paramedic grimaced when he examined Garrett's back, and dread washed over Laura.

The paramedics covered her mouth with an oxygen mask and took her vitals. As they wheeled her gurney toward a waiting ambulance, she reached out and grabbed Matt's arm. "Is Garrett okay?"

"He got badly burned," Matt said.

Before she could say anything else, she was loaded into the ambulance.

Matt climbed in, holding an oxygen mask to his mouth. He pulled it down a moment. "Third-degree burns," he reported. "The paramedic said the pain probably made him pass out."

A paramedic jumped in and closed the rear door.

"What about Garrett?" Laura cried. "You can't leave him." She tried to sit up but was seized by a coughing fit. She wasn't sure the paramedic even heard her through the mask.

"There's another ambulance," Matt reassured her. "Don't worry. They'll take good care of him."

Willing her coughing to stop, she prayed like she'd never prayed before. She could hardly stand to recall the anguish in Garrett's voice when she'd collapsed in the woods. It wasn't his fault. None of this was his fault. *I can't be the cause of someone else dying.* What had he meant?

"You really love him, huh?" Matt whispered.

She gaped at him. *Love?*

"Don't worry." Matt grinned. "The feeling is definitely mutual."

"Oh yeah," the female paramedic taking Laura's blood pressure said. "Any guy who'd run into an inferno like that to save you is a keeper."

Laura stared at them, uncomprehending. No guy had ever cared that much for her. Not even Mel, who'd sworn he'd love her forever. But he hadn't loved her enough to stay in Hopeton. And she supposed she hadn't loved him enough either, or she would've been willing to at least try to live in Pittsburgh.

"The heat was so intense, it felt as if I was driving into hell itself," Matt said, cutting into Laura's thoughts.

Laura swallowed. It was true. And Garrett had run into that for her. He'd braved his demons for her. And now he was fighting for his life because of her. What if he didn't know she was all right? What if he gave up because he thought he'd failed?

What if he didn't know she cared for him?

Laura's breathing quickened. Her head throbbed, and she felt horribly nauseated. But the instant the ambulance stopped, she sprang up—or tried to. The paramedic had strapped her to the gurney. "I have to get up." Laura clawed at the buckle. "I have to see Garrett." The coughing spasm started again, and her oxygen mask slipped.

The paramedic set it back in place. "You can see him after the doctor treats his burns."

"No." Laura found the latch and released the strap restraining her. "I have to see him now." She yanked off the tubes and lurched for the back door. "Open this door!" Her voice was so hoarse, she wasn't sure her order was comprehensible.

But the paramedic complied and helped Laura step down, then stood beside her as they waited for the doors of the other ambulance to open. The doors swung wide, and two paramedics emerged with Garrett's gurney between them. His skin was a bluish-gray that alarmed her.

"We've got to get him inside," one of his paramedics said to hers.

"Give her a second."

Laura clung to his hand. "I'm here, Garrett. I'll be waiting for you when you get out. I'm not going anywhere." Another coughing spasm gripped her, and the gurney started to roll toward the ER doors. Laura walked with it a few steps. "Do you hear me? I'll be right here. Waiting." She coughed again, doubling over.

Her paramedic grasped her by the shoulders and held her back so the others could wheel Garrett inside. "He'll be okay," she murmured.

A nurse pushed a wheelchair over to them and helped the paramedic get Laura seated. They reaffixed her oxygen supply.

"Do you think he heard me?" Laura asked anxiously.

"I'm sure of it," the paramedic told her.

Laura and Matt were taken straight to beds in the ER. A nurse drew samples of Laura's blood, and a doctor listened to her breathing and ordered chest X-rays.

"Will you want to intubate?" a nurse asked.

"It doesn't appear necessary." The doctor examined the readouts from the device the nurse had stuck on Laura's finger—a pulse oximeter, she'd called it—which tested the amount of oxygen in Laura's blood. "How's your throat feel?"

"Raw."

He nodded. "Your hoarse voice suggests there's damage to the respiratory tract. Intubating would ensure your airway doesn't swell closed and would allow us to suction any mucus that might develop, but unless you're sedated, it's quite uncomfortable. And your oxygen levels are already rising." He turned to the nurse. "We'll wait on the blood tests and radiology, but notify me immediately if there is any change in her condition."

By the time Laura returned from having her chest x-rayed, Matt had been released and her mother was waiting to see her.

Mom gave her a huge hug. "I'm so glad you're all right. You had us so worried."

"Where's Nancy?" Laura asked. "Have you heard how Garrett is?"

"Nancy's seeing him now. He's been admitted to the burn ward."

"But he's going to make it? He's going to be okay?"

Mom stroked Laura's arm. "Yes, I'm sure he is."

"It's my fault he got hurt. I can't believe he ran through the fire to save me."

Mom beamed. "You really care for this young man, and he seems to feel the same way."

Laura ducked her head. "I'm not sure how it happened."

"You finally opened your heart." Mom shook her head. "I never should've tied you to the diner. You'd probably already be happily married with a passel of kids by now. Or at least doing something you love."

"I love the diner," Laura insisted. "You know I do."

"What I know is that you loved your father, and you didn't want to see the last part of him we still had with us die too."

"But—"

"Stop." Mom held up her hand. "There's no point in arguing, especially when you have a sore throat. I was right there with you. Probably fed the silly notion in more ways than I care to remember." She smiled. "But now you have a chance at love."

Love. The word twined around her soul.

"I've been giving it a lot of thought," her mother went on. "I want you to sell the diner and start the garden design and nursery business you've always dreamed of building."

"What?"

"It's what you love to do, and doing what you love is the best way to honor your dad's memory. It's what he would've wanted for you. I see that now."

"Where is this coming from?" Laura asked, stunned.

"Talking with Garrett's mom. She was so enamored with your garden designs and how you lit up when you talked about plants. I realized that I've held you back from pursuing your passion all these years. And I'm sure being tied to the diner six days a week hasn't helped in the relationship department either."

Laura chuckled. "To be honest, that side of it is all on me." She swallowed in an attempt to moisten her throat. It hurt to speak, but she and her mom had never talked so openly. She needed to admit the truth before she lost her nerve. "I think seeing how much you hurt after Dad died, feeling that loss so deeply myself, and then having Mel choose the Pittsburgh PD over me—all of that made me not want to let myself care that much again. Hurt that much again."

Mom pulled her into a hug. "But the hurts are what make moments like these so special. This is life being lived. I'm sorry I didn't help you see that. I would never trade the love I had with your dad and the years we spent together for anything and certainly not to be spared the grief of losing him."

Emotions rolled over Laura like refreshing, glorious waves. "I think my feelings for Garrett sneaked up on me while I wasn't paying attention. He seems a bit controlling sometimes and that bothered me, but I think it's his reflexive way of coping with a situation that feels out of control."

"It is," Nancy said from the corner of the curtain. "You've come to understand my son perhaps better than he understands himself in the few short days you've known him."

Had it really only been a few days other than their brief encounter at the cemetery? It felt as if they'd lived a lifetime in such a short time. Was that what her mom meant by how she felt about her time with Dad? "How's Garrett?"

"Good," Nancy replied. "Still sedated. The doctor said his back will be painful for some time. He was more concerned about the degree of smoke inhalation. The exertion of carrying you out likely caused him to breathe in more deeply. It's apparently what kills most people caught in a fire."

"No!" Laura cried.

"Oh, don't worry," Nancy assured her. "He's out of the woods now. But there were some nasty chemicals in his blood—yours too, I imagine—not typical of a forest fire where no buildings are involved. They're thinking an accelerant must've been used to start it."

"Yes." Laura's pulse quickened with the sudden realization she hadn't reported Brad to the police. Which police officer could she trust?

The nurse came by to check on her, but before she said a word, Laura asked, "Can I visit Garrett's room?"

"I'll ask the doctor," the nurse said. A few minutes later, she returned with a wheelchair and a portable oxygen tank. "He said if you go in this and keep the oxygen on."

"I can push the chair," Nancy volunteered, and Laura's mom accompanied them. They exited the ER.

When Nancy turned the wheelchair toward the elevators, Laura spotted two officers—Lieutenant Reynolds and Officer Benson— entering through the hospital's front doors.

Her breath stalled in her throat. What if they were here to finish off her and Garrett before they even had a chance to start a life together?

"**G**o!" Laura urged as the elevator opened ahead of them.

Without hesitating, Nancy shoved the wheelchair forward.

Laura's mom hurried ahead of them and clamped her arm across the elevator door so it wouldn't close. "What is it? Who are those men?"

Nancy bustled them into the elevator and tapped the button for Garrett's floor.

"Cops," Laura hissed as the door closed.

"But they aren't in uniform," Nancy said.

"No." Which worried Laura even more.

"Maybe they came to ask you about the man who kidnapped you from the hospital," her mother suggested. "You should talk to them."

"I'm not ready to do that," Laura said.

"But—"

"I want to see Garrett." Laura hated herself for skirting around the truth. But what was she supposed to say? *I think they work for the guy who tried to kill us, killed Doc, and maybe kidnapped Caroline.* Caroline. Laura twisted in her chair. "I meant to have you call Caroline at her office. Do you have your phone?"

Mom handed Laura the phone as the elevator door opened.

"This way." Nancy wheeled Laura's wheelchair left, then right.

"That sign said fifth-floor geriatrics," Laura said. "I thought Garrett was in the burn ward on three."

"He would've been, but there were no private rooms available on the ward," Nancy explained. "After they learned he's Hopeton's new

GP, they wanted to ensure he's as comfortable as possible." She turned Laura's wheelchair toward the room at the end of the hall. "Here we are."

A nurse was in the room and asked them to wait outside the door until she'd finished.

Laura took the opportunity to call the senator's office.

The receptionist informed her Caroline wasn't in.

"Has she been in at all today?"

"No."

"Do you know where I can reach her?" Laura asked.

"I'm sorry, but I don't."

"May I speak to the senator?"

"I'll see if she's available."

She tightened her grip on the phone. "Tell her it's Laura Brennan."

A moment later, the senator picked up. "How may I help you?"

"Where's Caroline?"

"You sound upset. What's happened?"

"Where's Caroline?" Laura repeated.

"I'm afraid we haven't found her yet," the senator said. "I told you I'd call you as soon as we did. I assure you I have my best people working on it. Where are you?"

Laura abruptly hung up. She'd known Caroline's story on the phone this morning was a fabrication. Her cousin had thought someone was listening to their conversation. Who was it? Or had someone forced Caroline to make the call to get Laura to stop snooping? If that someone was the senator, surely she would've said Caroline was busy with a project or something. Otherwise, Laura would know something wasn't right.

The nurse exited Garrett's room. "You can go in now. He's awake."

Laura handed the phone back to her mom, and Nancy pushed the wheelchair into the room.

Garrett was propped on his side. His face was ashen except for the dark smudges shadowing his sunken eyes.

Laura pasted on a brave smile. "How's my superhero?"

"Better now that you're here." Garrett extended his hand. "Don't ever scare me like that again."

Laura slipped her fingers around his. She suspected the huskiness in his voice was a side effect of the smoke, but it was still endearing. "I'm afraid our troubles might not be over quite yet."

He tensed, his brow furrowing. "Did you tell the police about Carruthers?"

She second-guessed her instinct to tell him about Reynolds and Officer Benson downstairs. "No, I haven't talked to anyone. I still don't know who we can confide in."

A muscle in his cheek twitched.

Laura wondered if he was thinking about his friend Dr. Henri had tried to kill.

"I did learn something useful," Garrett said. "The doctors identified the chemicals in my blood." He paused, obviously finding it painful to talk. "One chemical in particular is a known by-product of burning industrial waste."

"The waste that leaked into the soil from the barrels?" Laura asked.

"That's what I'm thinking. The plants would've absorbed it, and when they burned, we inhaled the by-product."

"Would the presence of the chemical waste in the groundwater explain the mysterious symptoms so many people—like Herbert—have been experiencing?" Laura asked.

"Yes," he said. "And speaking of Herbert, my uncle wrote 'herb' on a receipt that he kept in his *Gray's Anatomy* textbook. I thought he'd been referencing a plant, but now I realize that he'd meant Herb MacKenzie."

"That makes sense," Laura said. "What are you going to do about the water?"

"I've already asked the doctor to contact public health about testing the well water in the area. If my theory is right, we should be able to reverse my patients' symptoms by getting them off the contaminated water and waiting for the chemicals to leave their systems."

"That's fantastic." Now they just had to ensure they lived long enough to act on the information. Laura told him about the arrival of Reynolds and Benson. With a sideways glance at their mothers, she stopped short of speculating why the officers were really at the hospital.

Garrett nodded as if he'd concluded the same thing. His thumb stroked the back of her hand.

At his touch, electricity hummed up her arm.

"We need to end this today," he said.

She startled at the harsh comment and jerked her hand from his.

Garrett recaptured her hand, his expression contrite. "I didn't mean end us." He bent his head toward hers and lowered his voice. "I meant the threat."

"How? For all we know, Carruthers has half the police force in his back pocket."

"You could go public," her mom suggested, apparently having caught on. "Your friend Zoe from high school is a field reporter for the local TV station."

"Or better yet, get in front of all the network TV cameras at once for a live press conference," Garrett said. "Tell the truth—or as much of it as we know—and leave it to the uncorrupted police to investigate. Once we expose the corruption, the dirty cops would have nothing to gain by silencing us."

"And they'd have all the more to lose," Laura added, "since another attack against us would only prove our claims. But how do we get the press here?"

"That shouldn't be difficult," Nancy said. "My son pulled you out of a raging inferno. Newscasters eat that stuff up. I'm sure all the network TV vans are already in the area to cover the fire."

"We should call Zoe's mom," her mother suggested. "See if she can convince Zoe to rally all the stations to come here for your story."

"In the meantime," Laura said, "how do we stay hidden from those two cops downstairs?"

"They won't check for Garrett on the geriatrics ward," Nancy said, "and I told the front desk I didn't want his room number given to anyone."

Laura wasn't sure what good that would do. She suspected cops had a way of insisting on compliance. She checked the clock and was shocked to see it was already past three. That meant the diner would be closed. "I could call the diner's cook to play bodyguard until after we talk to reporters."

"Tom?" Mom scoffed. "He's a teddy bear."

"Yes, but no one would know that from his appearance," Laura said. "Garrett needs someone to play interference if the wrong person decides to pay him a visit."

Garrett cringed, but he didn't argue, which told her how much pain he was in.

"Okay, call him, but I think we should talk to Zoe's mom first." Her mother handed her phone to Laura.

"I agree." Laura made the calls, then reported back to Garrett and their mothers. "She'll have Zoe text us when she's on her way, and Tom said he'd leave right away."

"Excellent." Laura's mom whispered something to Nancy, then said, "We'll wait by the elevators to watch for Tom."

Laura's stomach fluttered. She nibbled on her bottom lip as she returned her attention to Garrett.

He reached for her hand and folded his fingers around hers. "I'm glad you're okay."

"I have you to thank for that. I never would've made it out of there if you hadn't come after me. Thank you."

Garrett grazed his lips across her knuckles.

The flutters in her stomach erupted through the rest of her body.

"I couldn't have lived with myself if . . ." His voice trailed off.

When he didn't say anything more, Laura drummed up the courage to be a little nosy. "Back in the woods, you said, 'I can't be the reason another person dies.' What did you mean?"

Garrett swallowed hard. "It happened on my last tour of duty."

She squeezed his hand and nodded her encouragement.

Perspiration beaded his forehead, and his palm grew damp. "We were collecting casualties from a village that had been bombed. I treated a young boy who had shrapnel from an IED embedded in his leg. His mother, who had superficial wounds, didn't want to let him go to the hospital, but I was concerned the wound would get infected and he'd lose the leg. I insisted she let me take them to the hospital."

Laura touched Garrett's wrist with her fingertips, feeling his racing pulse.

"She convinced me to let her stay in the village by promising she'd keep the wound clean and bring him in at the first sign of trouble," Garrett said. "The boy begged me to take his mother to the hospital instead of him, not realizing her wounds weren't severe." He stared at their entwined hands. "God help me, against my better judgment, I left them both behind."

Laura's heart ached at the anguish in his voice. "What happened?"

"We'd scarcely left their street when another explosion erupted. We raced back, but we were too late. The boy and his mother were dead."

Was it any wonder he'd been so determined for her to do things his way? "You realize it's not your fault, right? I mean, you couldn't know another bomb would go off, never mind where. It could've just as easily been at the field hospital. Ultimately our lives are in God's hands."

He nodded. "More than once in the past few days, I've had to remind myself of that, thanks to your independent streak."

She grinned. "See, I'm good for you. You're making progress at working through this tragedy already."

"Yes." His lips trembled into a small smile. "You *are* good for me."

"Look who's here," Mom said, reentering the room with Nancy and Tom, who carried two steaming cups of coffee and set one on Garrett's bed table.

Laura's stomach rumbled at the delicious aroma. She glanced at the clock. Twenty minutes had passed, and it had felt like a lifetime and no time at all.

The nurse pushed through the door. "Dr. Simons needs his rest."

"We won't be much longer," Nancy assured her.

Zoe called to let them know she was on her way.

Moments later, the nurse came in again. "Are you Laura?"

Laura tensed. "Why?"

"The ER nurse wants to know where you got to."

Nancy dismissed the nurse with a flick of her wrist. "Tell her Laura will be right down. But Tom and I are going to sit with Garrett a little while longer."

"Fine," the nurse said and left the room.

"Garrett's staying here?" Laura blurted. "You're going to make me do the interview alone?" This wasn't how she'd pictured their plan going.

"Garrett is in no condition to be moved," his mother insisted.

"You can do this," Garrett urged Laura.

Of course, he had to pick now to give up being a control freak and let her lead the charge. Yet the certainty in his gaze stirred something inside her. Courage, maybe. She drew in a deep breath. "Okay, don't forget to turn on your TV."

The spurt of optimism was short-lived. Laura felt as if she were being wheeled to her execution as her mom steered her to the auditorium where Zoe had made arrangements for the impromptu press conference. She mentally rehearsed what she'd say, wishing she had time to write it down.

Zoe met them at the auditorium door and filled Laura in on how the Q and A would work following her initial statement. Then Zoe wheeled Laura onto the stage and introduced her to the crowd of reporters.

Laura realized that reporters weren't the only ones sandwiched into the room. Lieutenant Reynolds was leaning against the back wall, his arms crossed. Officer Benson stood by the exit.

Perspiration beaded Laura's forehead, but she reminded herself that at least if they were here, they weren't harassing Garrett.

"Good afternoon," she said into the microphone and jumped at the loudness of her voice. "Sorry."

Her mother gave her an encouraging smile.

"Yes, I wanted to talk to you today, because six weeks ago, I witnessed a hit-and-run accident. And this morning, right before tying me to a tree and setting the forest on fire around me, the driver of that vehicle, Brad Carruthers, admitted to me the hit-and-run accident was no accident."

The crowd gasped.

"Brad Carruthers, as you might know, is the son of Nathan Carruthers, the owner of PrimeCorp, a large manufacturing company here in Pennsylvania." Laura's throat ached, but she pushed on. "The victim of the hit-and-run accident was Dr. Richard London, a GP from Hopeton who'd been investigating the cause of a sudden outbreak of peculiar symptoms in his patients from south of town."

Conversation erupted in the audience as the attendees clearly got the gist of where this was going. Reporters shouted questions.

Zoe held up her hand and waited for silence. "Please let Laura finish. There will be time for questions at the end." She nodded to Laura to continue.

Laura opened the plant app she'd installed on her mom's phone and scrolled to the pictures Doc had taken of PrimeCorp's dump site. Handing the phone to Zoe, she asked, "Is there a way you can project those photos on the screen behind me?"

"You got it."

"What Doc discovered will be shown on the screen." Laura took a sip of water to ease the strain on her throat. "They are barrels of chemical waste illegally dumped by PrimeCorp in the woods south of town. The woods that were gutted by a forest fire this afternoon." She paused while Zoe slowly clicked through the photos.

"Brad Carruthers confessed his crime to me because he didn't expect me to live to tell the tale." Scarcely recognizing her own voice for the hoarseness, Laura recounted Brad's admission in detail, including his girlfriend's role.

Glancing Lieutenant Reynolds's way, Laura hesitated. So far, she hadn't implicated the police or the senator, but she knew she couldn't stop now. She drew in a deep breath. "I also believe Brad had my cousin kidnapped after she began to investigate PrimeCorp, and he has at least one police officer helping him cover up his crimes."

More chatter sent the noise levels in the room through the roof. Once again, Zoe asked for quiet.

Laura recounted her cousin's disappearance. "The man following her struck me from behind, so I didn't get a good look at him, but I did see the tattoo on his wrist. The same tattoo I noticed on a police officer's arm two days later when I tracked my cousin to a cottage on Lake Hopeton. Then the same police officer attempted to arrest me for a murder I didn't commit in an effort to cover his own role in all of this."

She glanced toward the police. Officer Benson squirmed, and Lieutenant Reynolds watched the other man curiously.

"I never found my cousin." Laura's voice cracked. She hoped her aunt wasn't watching this. "I believe she is still being held against her will, if she hasn't already been permanently silenced."

Several people in the crowd gasped.

"I asked for the opportunity to tell my story directly to the public because I didn't know if I could trust the police," Laura continued. "I've learned that PrimeCorp is a large contributor to Senator Funk's presidential bid. And my cousin works for the senator. I don't know if there's any connection between that and her disappearance, but the possibility concerns me." She swallowed the rest of her water, her hand shaking so badly it was a wonder she managed to get the glass to her lips.

Setting the glass on the podium, Laura said, "What I do know is that Brad Carruthers is willing to kill to ensure PrimeCorp's corruption isn't exposed. He admitted to killing Dr. London. If not for Dr. Simons's courage in coming to my rescue, Carruthers would've succeeded in killing me."

Lieutenant Reynolds pressed his phone to his ear, then walked out of the room.

Laura blew out a breath. "I'll take your questions now."

Reporters bombarded her with questions.

She answered them the best she could, but her voice soon started to give out.

Zoe joined her at the microphone. "We need to let Laura rest now. She's probably already strained her voice more than she should have after suffering smoke inhalation. We thank you for joining us today to hear her side of the story. I'm sure we're all looking forward to hearing from Brad Carruthers, the police department, PrimeCorp, and the senator to get their sides of the story."

The audience broke into applause, then quickly dispersed. Reporters moved to quiet corners where their camera operators could film recaps of Laura's speech.

Mom hurried onto the stage and enveloped Laura in a warm hug. "You did great." Her face was streaked with tears. "You're the bravest person I know."

Laura smiled and hugged her mother again. "Thanks."

Zoe wheeled Laura from the stage.

Lieutenant Reynolds stood at the bottom of the ramp, waiting for her. "You certainly know how to blow a case wide open. Good work."

Laura squinted up at him, wondering if he was for real or feeding her a line to save his own neck.

"I have a surprise for you." He handed her a tablet.

"What's this?" Laura gaped at the screen. "Caroline, where are you?"

Caroline beamed at her from the screen. "A safe house. I heard your speech. You did good."

"A safe house? Why didn't you tell me that this morning?"

"This morning, the feds warned me your phone could be tapped. To be honest, I wasn't sure I could trust the agents who claimed they were keeping me safe."

Laura glared at Reynolds. "You had her all this time?"

"No. After you mentioned Caroline's ex Sunday afternoon, I decided to check him out and found Caroline at his cottage."

Laura scanned the nearly empty auditorium, wishing a few reporters had stuck around. "If you're a good guy, why did you shoot Dwayne?"

"I didn't."

She studied him a moment before returning her attention to Caroline. "Dwayne said the bad guys took you."

"Because I thought Reynolds *was* a bad guy at the time. I didn't exactly leave willingly, and he did disarm Dwayne, but no shots were fired. I'm sorry I lied about the mob thing. Reynolds told me to implicate them to scare you out of investigating anymore, because he was worried you'd be targeted next."

"Then who shot Dwayne?" Laura asked.

Reynolds fielded the question. "I suspect Dwayne had a second gun in the cabin and made the mistake of drawing it on the next guy who walked through the door." He scrubbed his chin, clearly perturbed. "Based on your speech, I'm thinking that guy might've been Wes Benson, the cop with the tattoo."

"The cop you seemed to be more than a little chummy with here this afternoon," Laura pointed out.

"I found him outside the hospital when I arrived," Reynolds said. "It made me wonder if he was one of the senator's or PrimeCorp's minions, and I figured the safest course was to keep him close so I could watch him. Don't worry. I'm having him tailed as we speak. He won't get far."

The explanation was reasonable. But he was clearly a gifted liar, so how was Laura supposed to know if he was telling the truth now?

"If Officer Benson showed up at the cottage to find Dwayne wielding a gun," Reynolds continued, "he likely shot first and asked questions later. But proving it is another matter."

"Since his prints would be all over the place because of his answering my 911 call," Laura concluded.

"Right." Reynolds reached into his pocket.

Laura reflexively backed her wheelchair smack into her mother's midriff.

Reynolds held out his palms. "I'm showing you my ID." He presented an FBI badge and ID card.

"How do I know this is real? Thursday afternoon and every time I've seen you since, you claimed to be a police officer."

"I've been working undercover to investigate Senator Funk's dealings with the police concerning PrimeCorp," he explained.

"So she did strong-arm the police into making Doc's murder investigation go away?" Laura asked. "To make Caroline go away?"

"We have no proof of that," Reynolds answered.

Laura frowned at Caroline. "Do you think she's guilty?"

"I don't know. I don't want to believe it. Someone else in the office could've leaked to Carruthers the fact I'd been asking questions about PrimeCorp."

Deciding Reynolds was one of the good guys after all, Laura worried her bottom lip. "So, I kind of messed up your investigation, didn't I?"

"We suspect the senator is involved in other shady things as well," Reynolds said. "It's only a matter of time before we catch her. Your testimony against Carruthers will more than make up for the setback. I doubt Funk will remain in the presidential race after this scandal."

"What will happen to this cop with the tattoo who assaulted my daughter?" Laura's mom demanded.

"There will be a thorough investigation," Reynolds said. "With testimonies from Laura and Caroline and any other evidence that can place him at the house or in the vicinity that night, I'm sure his days on the force will be numbered. If we're lucky, we might be able to convince him to flip on the senator or PrimeCorp in exchange for reduced charges."

"He should pay for what he's done," her mom said.

"He will," Caroline assured her, as if she had the power to make it happen. "After the FBI has Carruthers in custody, I'll be free to go, and Laura and I are going to celebrate big-time."

Laura glanced back at her mother. "I need to tell Garrett about Caroline."

"We can go there now."

"The ER doc will be wondering what's happened to me," Laura said.

Lieutenant Reynolds shook his head. "I'm sure news of your press conference has reached the ER by now." He escorted them to Garrett's room.

At Laura's arrival, Nancy and Tom smiled broadly.

"You did great," Tom said.

Nancy echoed the sentiment, making way for Laura's mom to wheel Laura's chair next to Garrett's hospital bed.

Garrett beamed at her. "You're amazing."

Laura blushed. "This from the man who ran through a wall of flames to save me."

Garrett crooked his finger, beckoning her to lean in closer. "I think you should know that was purely selfish on my part." His gaze caressed her face. "I couldn't bear the thought of losing the woman I love."

Love. Joy burst through her. She curled her fingers around his. Was that what this feeling was?

Laura searched his exquisite blue eyes. She'd known Garrett for a few short days, yet he was the first person she thought of when she woke in the morning, when she had news to share, and when she was in trouble.

Fear edged into her chest. What if he got all controlling on her again when he wasn't lying in a hospital bed, racked with pain?

She drew in a ragged breath, remembering how he'd shielded her from the flames with his own body. And reminding herself that she now understood where his need to control the situation came from. She gazed into his eyes, faintly aware of the others slipping from the room.

His smile trembled.

Laura could feel her heart melting, which kind of scared her even more. On the other hand, he'd bared his soul and shared his dark secret with her. Unlike Mel, who'd only cared about what *he* wanted out of life, Garrett had encouraged her to follow *her* dreams. Dreams she hadn't given voice to for years, not until he'd asked her about them.

The lingering fear evaporated, and certainty lodged in its place. She squeezed his hand. "I love you too," she whispered.

Garrett's smile widened, his eyes crinkling at the corners and his dimples deepening. He tugged her closer and stroked her cheek. "You are so beautiful."

Laura felt her face heat up.

He slipped his hand behind her neck and gently drew her lips to his.

They were soft and tasted faintly of coffee. Surrendering, she reveled in the promise of his kiss.

"Maybe next time we can try this without oxygen tubes," he said.

She laughed. "Sounds like a plan."

Up to this point, we've been doing all the writing. Now it's *your* turn!

Tell us what you think about this book, the characters, the bad guy, or anything else you'd like to share with us about this series. We can't wait to hear from *you!*

Log on to give us your feedback at:
https://www.surveymonkey.com/r/sweetintrigue

Annie's FICTION

Inn at Magnolia Harbor

Enjoy Southern hospitality at its finest with sisters Grace Porter and Charlotte Wylde, co-owners of the picturesque Magnolia Harbor Inn. Joined by their eccentric aunt, Winnie Bennett, and their sweet shih tzu, Grace and Charlotte have built a new life running the beautiful inn, graciously providing a haven for those who need to get away from their hectic lives.

In each heartwarming story of the series, you'll love getting to know the charming residents of Magnolia Harbor, South Carolina, and the guests who are on journeys of the heart, ready to discover important truths about life and love during their stay.